Now You See Me

All rights reserved. This book or any portion thereof may not be reproduced or used in any manner whatsoever without the express written permission of the publisher except for the use of brief quotations in a book review.

ISBN: 9781794060746

This is a work of fiction. Names, characters, businesses, places, events, and incidents are either the products the author's imagination or used in a fictitious manner. Any resemblance to actual persons, living or dead, or actual events is purely coincidental.

Edits by: Tory Hunter & WB Welch
Cover art: Samantha Ransdell

*For Dad, Willie, and Taylor*

# Prologue

Seeing his brother for the first time in years was a blessing, but it was also a curse.

That was according to his father, anyway. Oliver didn't know where the *curse* part came into play, but his father saw it clearly.

"How could you do this, Levi?" His father ran his hand through his greying black hair. "Do you know what you've done to him?"

Oliver pulled his knees closer to his chest as he watched his brother's fists double. His brother just showed him a trick. That was all. It was only a trick.

"I didn't know he'd be able to do it," Levi took a step back. "I thought I was the only one who-"

"Apparently not," their father interrupted. "You've put a target on his back. How many more people are you going to drag down with you?"

Levi was silent; his tensed hands relaxed with a defeated sigh.

Oliver wasn't sure what his father meant. Nothing happened. Nothing. He and his brother were just playing.

"I guess I should go," Levi whispered. "Father, I'm sorry."

Their father said nothing, and Oliver could see his brother's eyes darken.

"Ollie, I'm sorry, I-"

"Don't talk to him," their father growled. "Just get out."

Tears streamed down Oliver's cheeks as he watched his brother trudge to the door.

"No," he whispered, but Levi didn't stop. "Please…"

He tried to force himself to run to his brother, but his knees were locked tight. It was too cold for Levi to leave in what little clothing he wore. He'd be shivering and all alone.

Levi turned one last time, but their father's glare shut him down. Within seconds, he was gone again. Gone along with all of the air in the room.

"Oliver."

He couldn't find his voice to answer back.

"Oliver, look at me."

When Oliver finally tore his eyes from the door, a chill ran down his back. His father's eyes were wild, afraid. They looked at him as though *he* was a deranged animal, but they were the ones who appeared almost primal.

"W-Where's Levi gonna go?" He was afraid to hear the answer.

"It doesn't matter, son. Listen to me." His father swallowed. "What your brother showed you - you can't do that. *Don't* do that."

"But father, I-"

He kneeled down and grabbed Oliver by the shoulders.

"Oliver, listen to me," his father's voice trembled. "Normal people can't do what you and your brother do. T-They'll be afraid if they know. They can't know."

"Levi didn't show me anything bad," Oliver formed a small flame in his hand. "Look. It's just fire."

He could see his mother in the doorway, her lightly tanned skin going pale. Her eyes were as wide as his father's, and, for a second, she looked as though she was going to faint.

"What have we done?" She fell to a kneeling position. "What have I done?"

The flame in his hand dissipated as he stared at his mother.

He felt the urge to go and comfort her, but something told him there wasn't anything he could do that would help. He and his brother had done something wrong, something that awakened a fear in even his father; someone he'd never seen waver in such a way.

"W-What if he gets the-"

"No, he can't. I..." His mother shook her head. "I don't know how..."

His father's hands fell to his sides, releasing the death grip he had around Oliver's shoulders. With each minute, his father's expression grew more and more barbaric.

"Charlotte," his father said. "Charlotte, what does this mean?"

"I-I don't..." His mom joined his dad in front of him. "Oliver, sweetie, you mustn't use your magic. Do you understand me?"

Oliver's eyebrows furrowed, and he looked down at his hands. They still looked the same; the same creases, same color, size... What were they so afraid of?

"Mom?" He asked softly as his mother brushed a strand of his black hair behind his ear. "Did I do something wrong?"

"No, baby," she said and put her forehead against his. "I did."

# Chapter 1

The twisted frown, wrinkled eyebrows, squinted eyes, and scrunched nose plastered on Oliver's face seemed to be a reflex every time he walked into the grand ballroom of the massive cruise ship. He didn't mean any harm, but he was aware of all of the wasteful activities happening around him. There was food all over the floor in various places, dropped by children - who were way too young to be on a *cruise,* by the way - who swung their arms back and forth as if having a seizure or conniption fit of some sort. Not to mention how messy the adults were, too. As they talked, they would gesture their arms in some absurd manner and fling their cheese, chicken, or broccoli behind them. They would then look to see where they dropped it at, proceed to giggle at each other, and go back to whatever dull conversation they were having before. There was no bother to pick it up, not with the money they were paying for their joyous vacation.

No, they let it rest on the floor with not a second thought in their mind as to how exactly that piece of food was going to make its way to the trashcan, which was not even five feet from their noses. Maybe it would get up itself and jump on in - grow legs, arms, a mustache, grab a hat and a cigar, and tip its hat to them before swan diving into its final resting place. That's what they seemed to like, after all. A show. Maybe he should give it a class on manners so that it could also please the guests just as he was supposed to-

"Oliver!" James, the head chef smacked him on the back of the head. "Stop dicking around and go tidy this place up a little. You know what Mr. Bain will do if he sees what a mess it is in here!"

Grumbling, he mustered up a nod before grabbing his broom, dustpan, and a damp rag. He hated it when it was his turn to clean the ballroom. Actually, he hated cleaning in general. At least he got to interact with some of the guests.

Well, when Mr. Bain wasn't in the room.

Oliver's eyes scanned the interior of the room. He hated cleaning but being in the ballroom always took his breath away. Its chestnut walls and light brown and red carpet went together perfectly. And of course, the one spot in the center of the room that was bare wood. There were several marks carved into it. They were all formed together in some mess that Oliver wasn't sure about, but over the years he'd come to appreciate it.

"Dear, I think my little Tommy here made a mess," a woman called to him, motioning him over with one finger. "If you could clean it up a bit."

"Of course, ma'am," Oliver said. "It's my pleasure."

The closer he got to the guests, the more their perfumes and cologne hit him. It was overwhelming.

He squatted to the floor to see the damage, which consisted of many *piles* of corn, and something mashed into the floor. Was that... a carrot? It was hardened and smeared, and no matter how hard he scrubbed and chipped at it, it wasn't coming up.

His eyes scanned the area, making sure that no one was staring in his direction before holding his hand over the spot and muttering under his breath. A tingling sensation that started in his fingertips, and within a second, the crusted food became saturated, and he was able to wipe it up easily with the rag. He once again peeked up, meeting the widened eyes of the toddler above him.

"Shh." He put his fingers to his lips.

The kid above him squealed as more of his corn rained on top of Oliver's head.

"Tommy, quit throwing your food." The woman whipped her dirty blonde ponytail over her shoulder. "I'm sorry, honey. He's just a little excited."

"It's not a problem at all." Oliver brushed the food from his hair. "He's a cute kid. How old is he?"

The smile on her face grew as she began filling Oliver's ear with every little detail she could think of since the day little Tommy was born. Her eyes were gleaming with each proud moment she listed, and Oliver could not help but become lost in the passion and love she was radiating. She had such a motherly aura, and it made Oliver feel warm and safe.

But he soon realized he had been listening to her talk for what felt like forever, and he hadn't gotten anything else done.

"Well, it should be sparkly clean around your table, ma'am. But let me take your plates, too." Oliver stacked their plates into his already full hands. "Let me know if you need anything else."

"Thank you so much," she said, and then pulled something from the pocket of her dark red pantsuit. "Here, for your troubles."

His eyes locked on the twenty-dollar bill she was beginning to slip in his hand.

"O-Oh, no thank you, ma'am, it's no trouble at all," he said, backing away as she continued to insist. "I'm not allowed to or else I would."

"You take this twenty, and it'll just be between us." She smiled, shoving it into his shirt pocket. "Now hurry on before someone sees, dear."

He stared at her for a second in wonder.

All of the guests were more than likely briefed in the beginning that they were strictly forbidden from tipping the workers on the boat, and in the three years that he'd been there, no one ever offered. He knew deep down that he couldn't keep it, but it was at least nice to feel appreciated.

The woman waved him away in a playful shooing motion, and he scurried back towards the kitchen as quickly as he could without putting the fine china he was holding in jeopardy. He knew better than to rush around like a fool holding valuables.

As soon as he opened the doors, he was met with helpful, steadying hands against the plates in his arms.

"Oliver, be careful!" James said, taking the plates from him. "These are brand new. You should've put your cleaning stuff down, *then* got these."

"Yeah, I'm sorry. I'll remember next time."

James stared at him for a couple of seconds before handing the plates to another worker. He then crossed his arms, and eyed Oliver up and down slowly.

"What?" Oliver squirmed under his gaze. "What's the matter?"

"You seem rather chipper. Especially for someone who hates cleaning," James said. "I saw you talking to that lady. You'd best be careful."

"No, no. She was just asking me to clean up is all. That's all."

*A whole twenty dollars.*

That was a lot of money. More than he'd ever had.

He wondered what he could buy with twenty dollars. Maybe when he went to deliver things from the ship, he could sneak to the shops and buy himself something. He could hide it under his mattress for a while so no one would see it.

"You sure?" James asked, and Oliver nodded. "Well, get ready to unload the cargo. We're almost to the dock."

"Where are we docking at?"

"Massachusetts."

Had it been seven days already? They all seemed to blend together after a while.

"Oliver, are you sure there's nothing else?"

"Nah, nothing. Honest."

Oliver made his way from the kitchen before James could ask him anything else. They were friends and everything, but James would rat him out to Mr. Bain in a heartbeat. Everyone was out for themselves, and everyone was looking for a way to get a leg up on the other. Be Mr. Bain's favorite.

He didn't care about Mr. Bain, though. He would rather spend his time in the shadows and not be noticed and scrutinized for every little move he made. In fact, in the three years he had been there, Mr. Bain only talked in his direction once every three months. Oliver wasn't even sure if he knew his name. It would always be 'come here, boy,' or 'hey, you, boy.' He would always reply, in his head of course, something he heard the guests say when someone called to them like that. Maybe something like "hay is for horses," or "I *do* have a name, you know," but he knew better than to say any of that out loud. Just thinking about it made him shiver.

Oliver stretched his long legs to their capacity with each stride he took, trying as best as he could to make it through the dining area fast. His eyes shifted around the room, scanning the area and people. No suspicious eyes, no odd movements, no-

He laughed at himself.

He was obviously feeling guilty about the money in his pocket. No one could possibly know he had it, though. No one was watching for that kind of thing.

"Hey, boy."

Oliver's breath caught in his throat as he froze mid step.

"Where are you off to in a such a hurry?"

*Turn around, turn around!*

Slowly, he turned, his eyes averted to the ground and his mind sighing at the sight of the perfectly spotless, shined, black dress shoes.

*Guess it's been three months.*

"I-I... James told me to get ready to unload the cargo, sir," Oliver said. "Do you need help with anything before I do so?"

When there was no answer, he peeked up and saw an uncharacteristic smile on the other man's face. Uncharacteristic, as in, he never smiled at his workers. It was the same, open-mouthed grin - the one that showed his pearly white teeth contrasted against his black skin - he gave the guests.

"James told me you did a good job tending to a woman and her child a bit ago," Mr. Bain smoothed his bangs up and out of his face. "Was she polite to you, boy?"

"Yes, sir."

"What all did she say?"

Again, Oliver peered up and observed the man's expression. He couldn't tell if James had ratted him out about talking to the guest, or if someone saw the woman tip him.

"She told me about her son and then thanked me for cleaning up. That's all, sir."

"Yeah?" Mr. Bain asked, and Oliver nodded. "I know you're lying to me."

Oliver winced as Mr. Bain's large hand wrapped around his wrist, and the next thing he knew he was being dragged into the other room, away from the eyes of the guests.

"Sir, I'm sorry," Oliver said. "I was going to give it to you. Honest-"

The slap across his face silenced him instantly.

"You know you're not supposed to talk to them, boy," Mr. Bain said, and then yanked the twenty from his pocket. "And you *know* you're not supposed to have this. What were you planning to do with it, huh?"

"I-I was going to give it to you."

"Were you going to buy yourself something nice?"

Oliver shook his head as he whimpered out a no.

He knew Mr. Bain was staring down at him, expecting some kind of excuse, but he didn't have one. They both knew that was exactly what he was going to do with it.

"Well, you're in luck. I have somewhere important to be, so you're off the hook," he said. "Don't let it happen again, *boy.*"

As soon as Mr. Bain was out of the room, Oliver could feel the air returning to his lungs. He should feel angry, he knew, but as he made his way downstairs, he merely shrugged his shoulders at the usual hostility surrounding him. Getting angry wasn't going to solve anything, and it definitely wasn't going to help his case.

# Chapter 2

Oliver grunted as he heaved the last of the luggage from the ship onto the ground. He had absolutely no idea what was in it, but if he had to guess based on the weight alone, probably a couple of animals.

Like maybe some sheep.

He grinned to himself at the thought. Nobody carried around animals in containers like that.

The warm breeze blew through his hair as he took in a deep breath. It was a rare occasion - him being by himself outside of the boat - so he took the opportunity to stretch as he watched the townspeople people bustle by.

The fact that each and every one of them had their own story, problems, and schedules was so enticing to him that he found himself constantly making up the narrative of their life. The way they moved or swayed as they walked, their posture… they all told so much about a person.

Like the lady to his right. As she walked her step had a bounce to it. Up and down and up and down. She more than likely had a good day at work or something. The man to his left, however, walked with his shoulders slumped and his chin tucked in. His boss probably fired him today, and he's wondering what he's going to do now that he-

"Stop standing there like a buffoon," a man said as Oliver's body was shoved effortlessly to the side.

Well, *some* people were interesting.

He glanced around for a second before muttering under his breath.

A stone from the sidewalk just in front of the rude man's feet popped up, and Oliver watched as he plummeted - kind of like a meteor - face first to the ground.

Oliver covered his face so he wouldn't laugh, but as the man pushed himself up off the ground, a loud giggle surfaced from Oliver's lips.

"Hey." The man was dusting off his blue buttoned up shirt. "Did you do that, kid?"

Even as Oliver shook his head, the man continued to stare at him.

"No, honest."

"Then what's so funny about me falling?"

Again, Oliver shook his head, and as the man neared him, he backed up.

This guy was shorter than him by a lot, but, with the way he was built, he might as well have dwarfed Oliver. His muscles protruded from his arms and chest like fat balloons, while Oliver's were more like... deflated ones. Or ones that weren't blown up at all.

"Nothing, sir," Oliver said, and felt his back against a wall. "I wasn't laughing."

"I think you were," the man said in his face. "Do you want to make a problem?"

"Um, no, I-"

Oliver's eyes widened as the man's right hand lifted, coming towards him open-palmed and in slow motion. He didn't know whether or not he should use his magic, because if anyone saw him, they'd be horrified. Or angry like that guy. But he didn't have time to think before an apple came flying from the table to his right, hitting the man's hand.

Oliver's eyebrows furrowed as both he and the man watched the apple fall to the ground with a hard thud.

"Did... Did you do that, too?" The man's face was a dark shade of red when he looked back up.

Oliver wanted to tell the man no, but he wasn't sure enough to say anything. He knew he didn't do it on *purpose*. But there was no other explanation for how it hit the guy so hard. The wind definitely-

A hand wrapped around Oliver's shirt as he was lifted from the ground and slammed up into the wall.

"You're going to regret-"

"Hey! Hey! You put him down right now."

Oliver looked up as the man turned, still holding him firmly in place, to see a short, curvy girl standing with her arms crossed. She wore baggy, blue jeans only held up by the black, leather belt around her waist, and a white tank top. Her hair, which was an aqua blue, came to a wispy end just past her ears, but was just long enough to cover her forehead and almost all of her thick, brown eyebrows.

"Do you know him?" The man asked.

"No, but I'm not going to let you pick on some kid," she said. "Put him down and get outta here. Mind your business."

Oliver's feet hit the ground as he heard the man snort and back away. He eyed the girl up and down and slowly made his way back in the same direction as before; over the stone sticking up in the middle of the path.

Oliver sighed as he leaned his head against the wall.

"Hey," the girl's voice cut through his relief. "Where'd you come from?"

"O-Oh, um," Oliver straightened up at her authoritative tone. "I'm from New Zealand."

"What? No, didn't you come off a ship or something?" She asked. "Like, that one over there?"

As Oliver looked over her shoulder to where she was pointing, the color drained from his face.

"Oh, shoot!" He said, watching the ship float away from the dock. "Oh, no. Oh, gosh."

"Look, it's alright, you can-"

Oliver took off running as fast as he could, stripping his socks and shoes off as he went. His mind was racing, so he didn't even hear the girl calling after him.

"Hey, hey!" She grabbed his arm. "What are you doing?"

"I gotta get back on that ship. Oh, god, Mr. Bain's going to kill me."

Her hand held him firmly in place.

"So what, you're just going to swim after it?"

"Yes."

"You're going to-" she yanked him backwards when he tried to pull away. "The hell you are! And then what?"

No matter how hard he pulled, her strength was enough to hold him still.

"You don't understand," Oliver said. "I work on that ship."

"Yeah, but you're not going to swim to it! Chances are they wouldn't even see you," the girl said. "When's it getting back?"

"Seven days."

The girl sighed as she jutted her hip out and placed her hand atop it.

"Do you have anywhere to stay? How old are you?" She asked. "You obviously can't stay by yourself."

"Well, I'm eighteen," Oliver said. "But I've gotta get back-"

"You're *eighteen?*" She asked, and he nodded. "But you're so little."

He looked down at himself.

The oversized, brown sweater he wore swallowed nearly his entire upper half, and his equally loose jeans took care of the rest of him. He would admit that he *appeared* little in terms of meat on his bones, but he was sure he was nearly a foot taller than her.

"I-I need to get back to-"

"You can't go after the boat," the girl interrupted. "Come on. You can stay in my dad's hotel while you wait."

Releasing his arm, she began making her way back in the opposite direction.

Oliver's eyes went to the boat, which was still slowly drifting away from the dock. Now that he was looking at it, it was a little far away. And who was even going to see him if he was able to catch up? Using his magic was an option, but he only knew a few spells. None of which would be much help.

Plus, he might die if he tried to go after them. All the sharks, jellyfish, and blowfish... oh, god the *blowfish*.

"H-Hey!" Oliver said, running after her. "Hey, wait up!"

"Come on, I don't got all day," she said. "What's your name?"

Even though she was shorter than him, her pace had him running to keep up.

"Oliver. You?"

"Lynn," she said. "So, *Oliver,* you must have a pretty important job on the boat if they forgot you. What do you do?"

"Well, a lot of everything," he said. "But, um, I don't think I can stay at your dad's hotel."

She turned to him with a leveling glare.

"Why not?"

"Well, I don't have any money," Oliver said. "That's why I need to get back to the ship."

If he had been able to keep that twenty from before, maybe he could pay for the whole week. He didn't know what the rate for hotels was around there, but surely it would've covered something.

"You don't have any money?" She asked. "What, they don't pay you on the ship?"

"Um, no," Oliver said. "I'm not allowed to have any."

Lynn wrinkled her nose as they continued on.

"Isn't that illegal?"

Oliver shrugged his shoulders. His payment, as well as the other workers, was Mr. Bain not outing them to the public about their magic. They were told if the American government were to find out, they would be gone in a heartbeat. He wasn't too sure, but he complied anyway.

"Well, you must be good at something," Lynn said. "Maybe you can work around the hotel to pay for your bill until your boat gets back. What're you good at?"

He had his magic. He wouldn't say he was particularly *good* at it, but it was something no one else around here probably had.

"There's one thing, um," he looked over at her nervously. "But I'm not supposed to tell anyone at all I don't think."

"What do you mean?" She asked. "Just tell me."

His mom and dad said that he shouldn't ever use his magic, and Mr. Bain said people would be horrified if he told anybody. And after dealing with that angry man, he wasn't sure he should even tell her. But she seemed nice enough. A little intimidating. But polite.

"Well," he whispered. "I-I have magic."

When she stopped, her face was not as surprised as he thought it would be. In fact, it held the same semi-bored, raised eyebrow expression she had from the beginning.

"So you're a magician?"

"A-A magician?" He laughed, but she just stared at him. "Oh, you're serious. Um, yeah, I guess. A magician."

"Well, if you want you can perform in the lobby or something," Lynn said. "I'm sure dad would be okay with that."

For the next couple of minutes, they walked in silence. He wondered, as he peeked over at her, what exactly she was thinking. The look on her face made it seem like she smelled something foul;

her nose was wrinkled, her mouth was twisted... he leaned over his shoulder to smell his shirt.

"What are you doing?" Lynn asked, and then shook her head. "So, do you like working on the boat?"

"Um, I don't know. It's okay I guess," he said. "Mr. Bain is a serious guy. He gets mad at us a lot so it's kinda stressful."

Since he was thinking about it, he wasn't sure what he thought about his work. It was kind of just something he did every day because he had to. What else would he do, after all? Mr. Bain wasn't going to let them just sit around.

"Then why would you even want to go back?" Lynn snorted, shoving her bangs from her eyes. "Doesn't sound like any fun. If I were you, I'd look at this like a sign."

"A sign?"

"Yeah, like, maybe you should be doing something else. Something you'd enjoy," she said. "You said you're a magician. If I were you, I'd go to New York or LA or somewhere and make it big. Be a star."

Be a star? He didn't know what she meant by that, but it sounded nice.

"Are New York and LA close?"

"Oh, that's right, you're from New Zealand," she said. "New York's pretty close. Like four hours. LA's on the other side of the US."

Oliver glanced around at the buildings as they passed them. Some were small, but some were so gigantic he had to crane his neck back. He'd always see them from the boat, and they looked huge, but up close, it was insane. It was like nothing he had ever experienced before.

"So what do you do?" He asked. "Do you work in one of these big buildings?"

"No, but you're going to break your neck if you stretch it back any further," she laughed as he dizzily pulled his head back to level. "I work in my dad's hotel. I guess my job's kind of monotonous like yours. Except *I* haven't gotten a sign yet."

He watched her sigh as they continued into the city, their pace slower than before. Her face was different, he noticed, but he had never been too good at reading expressions, so he decided to stay quiet the rest of the way to the hotel.

When they arrived, nearly walking into a door that opened by itself, Oliver was rushed with the sound of familiar instrumental pieces that were usually played on the ship. He fought back the urge to wrinkle his nose in the case Lynn was watching him. Everything else about the hotel - the dark red, plush carpeting, the black walls, the strong smell of disinfectant - was great. It was a clean, well-kept building.

"Hey, you. Glad you're home!" A man at the front said. "I know you worked all morning, but I've got this thing I need to take care of, so I'll need you to take the desk for the night."

Oliver heard Lynn sigh.

"Dad, I can't," Lynn said. "I'm helping someone out right now."

Her dad turned his attention to Oliver.

Oliver could tell where Lynn got her disinterested, scrunched up expression from, because as her dad looked him up and down, there wasn't even a hint of enthusiasm on his face.

"And who are you?"

"Well, my-"

"His name's Oliver," Lynn said. "He works on a cruise ship and it left the dock before he could get back on. So, he's stuck here for a week."

Her dad was a tall man with short, brown hair and a pudgy build. His fingers, which drummed on the desk with each tick of the clock, were so big it looked as if he was suffering from an allergic reaction.

"Oliver, huh? Well, the name's Mason. A week'll be pretty expensive," her dad said. "Do you think you'll be able to pay for it, or will you have to have your parents-"

"He's a magician, so he's going to perform in the lobby," Lynn interrupted. "I thought that'd be enough to cover the bill. He says he doesn't have any money."

"A magician? That's pretty neat."

Lynn and her dad stared at each other for what felt like forever.

"Well, if he's going to perform, then you'll be here to run the front," he said, and Lynn groaned. "What? Honey, I've got stuff I need to do."

"Let me go set things up in the corner for him, and I'll be right up," Lynn snapped.

Oliver stepped out of the way quickly as she stormed past, her fists clenched.

"Short temper," Mason laughed. "So, Oliver, do your parents know where you're at? Are they on the boat? They're probably worried."

"O-Oh," Oliver said, rubbing his arm. "They're probably fine, I mean-"

"No, no," Mason said, and then started fumbling around on the desk. "Here, I'm going to go in the back for a sec. Why don't you give them a ring?"

Before Oliver could argue, Lynn's dad shoved a landline in his hand and disappeared through the doorway.

Oliver bit his lip as he stared down at the phone. Their town had one like this in a tiny shed in the middle of the square, but barely anyone was allowed to use it. He remembered going in with his mom one time when his father was gone. She said she wanted to call Levi, his brother, but as soon as she picked it up, his father came home.

Sighing, he put the phone up to his ear.

He knew he couldn't call his parents, and the low-pitched, steady tone seemed to emphasize that fact. It was loud and blaring as he continued to just stand there and listen, squeezing his eyes shut in an attempt to make it stop. It made his chest hurt and his body feel heavy. Almost too heavy for his legs to support.

As Mason returned, Oliver turned his back, mumbling a couple of words under his breath so it sounded like he was talking to someone.

"Yeah," Oliver said softly. "I… I miss you, too, Mom. Bye."

"I knew it was a good idea to call," Mason said, taking the phone back. "If Lynn was in this situation, I'd want her to."

Oliver nodded.

His dad was worrisome like that, too. Anytime Oliver went anywhere, his dad always had to know. Especially after Levi left. He wasn't sure if it was because his father was nervous about his magic, or whether or not he'd go running off after Levi.

"Okay," Lynn said. "It's all set up, Oliver."

"Thanks, sweetie," Mason said, coming around the counter. "Now, I gotta split. Call me if you need anything."

Mason was out of the door before anyone could say anything thing else.

"Your dad seems pretty nice," Oliver dared to say, receiving a glare from Lynn. "N-No, really. He seems like he really loves you."

"Yeah," Lynn sighed. "I guess I just… well, he's always shoving things off on me. I never get to have any fun because I'm always picking up his slack."

Oliver stared down at the desk as a customer came in.

He knew how she felt. He was always doing things for Mr. Bain with no appreciation in return. In fact, Mr. Bain had never said thank you the entire time he'd worked for him. At least Lynn's dad genuinely cared for her; Oliver could tell by the way he talked about her.

"Thanks, enjoy," Lynn said to the customer, then turned her attention back to Oliver. "I dunno. Maybe I'm just being a crybaby. I just feel like there's something more…"

"Then why not go do something?" Oliver said. "You told me to take my boat leaving as a sign. Shouldn't you take your feelings as one, too?"

Lynn shrugged her shoulders at him, blowing her bangs out of her eyes as she plopped her chin down into her hand.

"If you want to make some money performing you should go ahead and get started," she said. "Rush's about to start."

Oliver looked down at his hands before nodding. He was about to use his magic *in front of people*. And they were going to be aware of it. How were they going to react?

***

Oliver looked around nervously at the small crowd gathering in front of him. He probably should have figured out what kind of tricks a magician did before he agreed he was one.

What were they expecting from him?

"Um," he gritted his teeth together. "H-Hello, my name's Oliver Lee. I guess I'm here to be a magician today."

They all just stared at him, their gazes like ice.

"Okay, so…" He felt his arm brush against the plant beside him. "Oh! Oh, well, I guess I'll just show you something with this."

He plucked a small leaf from the plant and laid it in the palm of his hand. The crowd was still staring him down with the same bored expression Lynn seemed to have permanently carved into her face. Maybe it was just a Massachusetts thing.

The leaf in his hand began to smoke, and with one quick word under his breath, it burst into a tiny flame, melting the gazes before him.

"Oh, wow!" He heard a kid say. "Mommy, mommy, how'd he do that?"

This was actually pretty cool. No one was looking at him like Mr. Bain or his dad said they would. Actually, they all looked… impressed.

"Does anyone have a piece of paper I could borrow?" Oliver asked with more confidence. A man handed him a small, folded up paper. "I'm going to make it float between my hands."

He heard a couple of whispers as he smashed the paper between his hands, and the next thing he knew, as he lifted the one on top, there were gasps.

The folded-up paper was floating before him, sending a chill down his back.

What was that feeling?

He was smiling - laughing almost - as he removed his top hand from the still levitating paper. The stress and tension, the very things that felt like threads holding him together, were beginning to leave his body.

"Here," Oliver said, bending down to one of the kids in front of him. "You try."

He placed the paper in the wide-eyed child's hand and sealed it from the top with his own. Softly, he counted down from three to one, and as he once again lifted his hand, the paper came with it, floating just above the boy's finger tips.

"Mommy! Mommy!" The boy squealed. "Mommy, look!"

Oliver stood up, taking the paper with him.

It was... amazing. He had never felt like that before in his life.

He spent the next several minutes doing variations of the previous tricks, all amazing the patrons just as much as the last.

"We're going to take a short break," he said sheepishly as everyone clapped. "Thank you."

He turned towards the front desk, where Lynn was, and he could see her smile. She had been working with a customer through most of that, but from the new way she looked at him, he could tell she saw it all.

"Oliver," she said as soon as he made it over. "How did you do that? That was so cool!"

"Magic," Oliver said with a grin. "They were all wrong when they said people would be scared."

When Lynn said nothing back, he turned, catching the tail end of what was the probably the most enormous eye roll he'd even seen. When she noticed him staring her, eyebrows furrowed, she gave him a quick grin.

"You magicians," she said. "So secretive. I hope you know I *will* find out how you did it. No one keeps secrets from me."

"N-No, I'm serious, I really-"

"Lynn. Lynn, are you...here?"

Before he turned, Oliver watched the color drain from Lynn's face. He looked over his shoulder to see Mason stagger his way through the doors, nearly falling into the trash can to his right.

"Dad? Oh my god," Lynn groaned. "Dad, what the fuck?"

"I had some... business to take care-" her dad put his hand to his stomach.

"Shit, dad, don't throw up. Let me get the-"

Oliver mumbled under his breath. The trash can slid in front of Mason just as he began puking. He had to turn his head so he didn't do the same.

"That's some cool magician stu-" her dad continued to heave out his insides. "Oh, god."

"I thought you had *business* to do," Lynn said. "Dammit. I can't leave the desk. You're just going to have to find your own way to your room."

Mason hung over the trash can for a couple of seconds before lifting his head.

"I don't think I can stand," he mumbled.

Oliver could practically see Lynn's teeth grinding.

"I-I can help him," he said. "You stay up front, and I'll help him to his room. It's the least I can do."

"Oliver, you don't have to-" a customer came walking in. "Okay, okay. It's down that hall. Third room."

Oliver heaved the man, with much difficulty, up off the ground. He was heavy, and each time he staggered to the side, he would bring Oliver with him, nearly knocking the both of them over.

"You-You're a good kid, uh, what's your name again?" His breath was stale.

"It's Oliver." He opened the door to the room. "Here we are, Sir. Be careful don't-"

Oliver's eyes widened as Mason let go of him and began falling towards the glass coffee table. Without thinking, he threw his hands forward, and in almost slow motion, he watched the table glide to the side; the bed slid over to replace it.

Mason hit it with a thud, and within seconds, Oliver could hear him snoring lightly.

Oliver sighed, putting his hand to his head in silent relief. That was way easier than he expected. He had to deal with drunk people on the ship every once in a while, but they were always difficult to manage.

Before he could start back towards the door, a warm, blistering sensation warmed his chest. At first it was bearable, but as seconds ticked by, it got worse and worse until-

"Ah," Oliver ripped his shirt off as fast as he could. "What the…"

He tugged the skin from his collarbone down as best as he could so he could better see the foreign mark on his skin. It was a dark black line, almost as if he had been burned, but as he traced it with his finger, it was the same temperature as his skin. On the outside, that is. It still burned ever so slightly on the inside.

It wasn't there before, but its color… something about it seemed familiar.

He walked over to the dresser and stared at the mark in the mirror. Where had he seen it before? The way the line curved up at the end and thinned out…

"Oliver," Mason mumbled, rolling over. "Make sure you call your parents. You never know when you won't be able to anymore."

Oliver stared at Mason's reflection in the mirror to see if he was awake, but it seemed as though he was out once again. Even though Lynn didn't think so, she and her dad were lucky to have each other. Her dad really loved her, even if he did make mistakes.

He slipped his shirt back over his arms before covering Mason with the blankets he wasn't on top of.

"I know, sir."

Oliver closed the door behind him as quietly as he could.

# Chapter 3

Oliver watched from the hallway as Lynn gazed out into the empty lobby. She had her chin propped up against her fist, her eyes drooping. Her other hand tapped on the desk to the tick of the clock, like her father's did, but the slower her eyes began to blink, the more delayed her tapping became.

Finally, without warning, her forehead hit the desk, sending out not only a loud thump through the vacant room but also a groan.

"Lynn?"

She gasped as she snapped her head up.

"O-Oliver?" She said. "What are you doing? You scared me."

"I'm just watching you," he said. "You can tell a lot about a person by watching them."

She stared at him, her autumn colored eyes sending a wave of warm serenity through his body. For some reason, and he didn't understand why, he felt relaxed around her. From the very moment they met, he felt a sort freeness to his mind that he hadn't ever experienced.

"Yeah? What can you tell about me?"

"Huh?"

"What kinda reading did you get from me, Mr. Tarot Card?"

A giggle surfaced from her lips when his face reddened.

"O-Oh, um, well, I normally keep that kinda stuff to my-"

"No," Lynn said with a smile. "Tell me. What did you see?"

The lobby around them had grown quiet. The late-night stragglers had migrated to their rooms, and the teenagers down the hall opposite of Mason's room had more than likely fallen asleep - judging by the absence of their booming music.

"Well, you're really strong. And kind," Oliver said, rubbing the sore spot near his collarbone. "But… you're lonely, I think. You're lonely and even though you find interest in everything around you, you don't find it in yourself."

Lynn's mouth was wide open when he looked up.

"I'm probably wrong, though," Oliver said quickly. "A-About the lonely stuff. I think the stuff before that's... true."

He watched her face as she stared down at the desk. He figured she was processing, but something in the back of his mind told him he shouldn't have mentioned anything.

"No, it's all true," Lynn finally said. "I guess I just feel... like, what's even interesting about me? I went to school, graduated, and I've been working here since. I haven't traveled, partied... I'm just... existing. Rotting away."

It was quiet again as they stared into each other's eyes. Oliver wasn't sure what to say, but for some reason, he didn't feel like he needed to speak. It wasn't until her eyes darted down, breaking the spell that kept his gaze on her, did he even begin to think again.

"Then let's do it," Oliver said, grabbing her hand. "You're right."

"What're you talking about?"

As soon as he realized what his hand had done, he pulled it away, scratching the back of his head.

"I mean, why would I wanna go back to my dumb, stupid, boring job?" Oliver laughed. "Let's... I wanna to go to New York like you said."

Lynn's smile grew as she slapped the desk.

"Well, all right!" She said. "I think you should."

"No, I want you to come with me."

"Wait, really?"

Getting to New York by himself would be hard, he knew, especially since he had no idea how to even begin. But Lynn appeared to be pretty smart, and something told him maybe they both needed the trip.

"Yeah," he nodded. "Let's go to New York. Together."

Lynn's eyes lit up as she practically bounced up and down before him. That was more emotion than he'd seen from her all day.

"Okay. Okay," she said. "Just watch the desk for a couple of seconds for me, and I'll come get you. No one's going to come in. Just give me a bit, okay?"

He watched in amusement as she darted around the desk and out the front door.

They were going to *New York*.

He bit his lip as the excitement inside of him grew. It had been a long time since he'd had something to look forward to. No longer was he going to go to sleep just to get up and do the same thing the next day.

For the first time in three years, he didn't know what was going to happen.

***

"This way," Lynn hissed, leading him into an alleyway. "Oliver, come on."

They came to a beige, boxy, beat-up looking machine.

"This is a car," Oliver said, but it almost sounded like a question. "I've never been in one before."

Lynn's eyebrows scrunched together in their seemingly usual look.

"You're joking," she said, and he shook his head. "You've never been in a car? They don't have cars in New Zealand?"

"Well, they do, but not where I'm from," Oliver pulled open the door. "We saw lots of them, but my dad never let me get in one."

Plus, they never looked so… old. Some of them were a little aged and beat up, he would admit, but he didn't think he'd ever seen one that rusted and out of shape. He wasn't sure if it was even capable of turning on.

Lynn closed her door and turned on a light on the roof.

"Okay, so, this might take a little while," she said. "I've gotta hotwire it."

"What? Are-" he shook his head. "Are we stealing this?"

"Well, yeah."

He watched in awe as she struggled for the next few minutes with no success. Finally, she threw her hands up with a frustrated sigh.

"Dammit, I must've done this a hundred times."

"Can I try?" Oliver asked, and she glared at him. "No, really, I think I can do something."

After his older brother Levi left their hometown, again, he went to a college in Germany for electrical something or another. Oliver could remember his brother telling him all kinds of things about how electricity worked and even showing him a trick - secretly, of course, with his magic. However, the lesson was very short lived after their father found out.

He watched as Lynn placed her hands on either side of her head, rubbing her temples. Her eyes were closed as she mouthed something to herself for what felt like forever.

"No, *Merlin*," she finally said. "You've never been in a car."

"Merlin?" He asked, watching her grab at the wires. "What do you mean?"

After she pulled out a pair of pliers and ran them against a couple of the wires, stripping their color away, she twisted them together, bringing the lights on. Then, she stripped another, sparked the wires, and the engine roared to life. She revved it a couple of times before grabbing the wheel and jerking it to one side.

"Yeah, you know. The wizard guy," Lynn said, and Oliver tilted his head. "Oh, no I guess you wouldn't know. Never mind."

Lynn pulled the stick in the middle backwards, and the car started to move, much to Oliver's surprise.

"Wow," Oliver said as they pulled onto the road. "It's so fast."

"Yeah. That's why it only takes four hours to get to New York instead of three days," Lynn said with a smirk. "Are you sure your boss is going to be okay with you just disappearing? He's probably already noticed you're gone."

Oliver looked down at his hands and stared blankly at his fingertips.

"No, Mr. Bain'll probably never know I'm gone," he whispered. "They'll do just fine without me. What about you?"

"Me?" Lynn snorted. "Huh. Well, dad'll be fine I'm sure."

*Mr. Bain* would probably never notice his disappearance, but James and the other workers would eventually. He probably had at least a couple of days before anyone said anything to each other. Then, one of them would bring it to Mr. Bain's attention. He didn't know what would happen after that, since no one had ever left the ship, but it couldn't be good. No one got one up on Mr. Bain.

"How did you end up on that bore-fest anyway?" Lynn asked. "You don't make any money, you don't have fun… I mean, I would've left when I found out there wasn't any pay."

If only he had the option. He would've loved to run off that ship as fast as he could when they docked the first time. They kept him pretty much locked up for the first couple of months. He couldn't remember the first day vividly, but he *could* recall that Mr. Bain was looking for something, even before he got him on the ship.

*"Strip him down."*

*Oliver's widened eyes locked on the two younger men walking towards him, and then flashed back to his father, who was being held firmly in the corner of the room.*

"Dad?" Oliver said, backing away. "Where's-"

"Son, just do as he says, alright?" His dad struggled against the men holding him. "Where's Charlotte? Where is she-"

The dark colored man stepped towards Oliver's dad, and, without hesitation, slammed his fist into his stomach.

"You all made it too easy this time." The man leisurely made his way over to Oliver. "I found her and her daughter, but she has two kids, doesn't she?"

The cold air hit Oliver's naked body as he was stripped of everything but his underwear.

"There's not one here, sir."

"What?" The man said, turning Oliver in a circle. "No, I've seen it. Levi, did your mother-"

"No, my name's Oliver."

The man's glare made Oliver squirm.

"What's the meaning of this?" The man asked. "This is a younger brother?"

"No, okay? We adopted Oliver."

Oliver's eyebrows furrowed. He knew he wasn't adopted. He had the same skin tone, eye color, and hair color as his mom. Why was his father saying these things? Who was this man?

"Where is he?"

Oliver hugged his clothing to his body as he began to shiver, but he couldn't tell if it was from fear or the cold.

"I don't know what you're-"

The man picked Oliver up by his throat, squeezing tightly.

"D... Dad..." Oliver kicked his feet as hard as he could, but it did nothing to phase his captor.

"He's gone! He left!" His father said. "P-Put him down!"

Oliver fell to the ground with a loud thud.

*"He might not have it, but I can feel his magic," the man said. "I'm taking him with me."*

"Oliver?"

Oliver's eyes fluttered as he was knocked out of his daze. He wasn't in his home or with his dad, but in a car with an almost complete stranger who for some reason agreed to go with him to New York.

"Um," he shook his head. "Right. The ship. Leaving was just kind of complicated."

"That's it?" Lynn asked, but Oliver stayed quiet. "Well, I guess you had your reasons."

It was silent as they drove. Oliver continued to stare down at his hands, but he could see Lynn sneaking quick looks over in his direction.

"You know," Lynn said, breaking the silence. "I stayed at my boring job for a reason, too."

"Yeah?"

"Mhm. I, uh-" her voice caught, and Oliver turned to her. She was chewing on her lip, gripping the steering wheel tightly. "I've had a little bit of a... drug problem."

The air around them had become tense, and for a second, Oliver wasn't sure whether or not she was angry or almost in tears. She sniffled a little, but there weren't any tears rolling from her eyes.

"I, uh, guess I didn't fall far from the tree. My dad - as you saw earlier - is basically an alcoholic. My mom... she overdosed on heroin," she continued. "I dunno. I was stressed, I tried it a couple of times, and it made things better. For a while."

"Only a while?" Oliver asked, and she nodded. "Then what happened?"

"It stopped making things more vibrant than they actually are. I started having to use more."

He watched as a tear rushed down her cheek and just below her chin.

"I knew it was wrong. I mean, that's how my mom died," Lynn said. "After almost getting shot by another druggie, I knew it was time to stop. I stayed there because buying and selling was easy at a hotel, but that's why I needed to get out."

He wanted to take his sleeve, just as his mother used to do with him, and wipe her tear away; to reach out and squeeze her hand in comfort, but he...

"That's pretty fucked up, huh?" She laughed, rubbing her arm across her face.

"We all make mistakes, you know," Oliver said. "It's okay...to do stuff that seems unreasonable. I think it's just human nature to be curious."

Her sniffles were more pronounced now. She was trying to make it look like she wasn't upset - she would clear her throat or pretend to stretch her arm towards her face - but not only could he see it, he could *feel* it.

Oliver could feel his hand moving towards hers, but he was trying his hardest to resist. She didn't need him to comfort her. She was strong - way stronger than he was. If anything, he would probably make things worse. He always did.

"It..." His fingers wrap around her cold, stiff hand, relaxing it almost instantly. "It's okay, Lynn."

"I haven't had anything in a couple of months, but the craving's still there," she whispered. "I-I'm afraid I'm gonna fall back in... And then what?"

Oliver squeezed her hand tighter. He didn't know much about drugs, since where he came from was all about natural medicine, so he didn't know what to say. He felt... helpless. Just as he did the day Mr. Bain took him away. Just as he had for the last three years.

"I'm sorry. That was a lot of, um, " Lynn pulled her hand away to scratch her head. "It's a lot to take in."

"I don't mind," Oliver said. "I like listening to you talk."

He wrinkled his nose at that last statement he made.

"That's a relief," Lynn said with a smile. "It's nice to have someone who isn't repulsed by-"

Oliver's eyes widened as a large figure - right as they swung around a curve - leapt into the car's small line of vision. He didn't have time to speak before the car squealed as loudly as it could, trying desperately to-

*"Don't tell dad I'm showing this, yeah?" Levi said, pulling the wagon up the hill. "It's nothing too useful, but it might come in handy. Actually, it's just really funny to do to people in the big cities. Like Greymouth."*

*Oliver nodded as they finally made it up the hill.*

*"Come on, show me!" He said, clapping his hands. "This is going to be so super cool-"*

*"Shh! Someone's going to hear!" Levi covered his brother's mouth. "Okay, look. I'm going to push this thing down the hill. Let's say you want it to stop. Put your hands out, focus your energy, and just say stop."*

*Oliver wrinkled his nose. That seemed a little too simple. All the other magic his brother taught him had some complicated name to say.*

*"Yeah, yeah, I know. Pretty simple, right? Now watch." Levi shoved the wagon down the hill and pushed his arms forward. "Stop."*

*The wagon came to a halt immediately. No resistance. No skidding. It was as if his brother had a stronger hold on it than gravity.*

"Wow," Oliver said. "Now I'll try!"

"Now remember," Levi said. "Arms forward. Then you just say-"

"Stop!"

If it hadn't been for the seatbelts around their bodies, they would've both went flying out of the window. The car stopped instantly, just inches away from the large doe crossing their path.

The animal looked at them for a second, its eyes reflecting back an ominous green, before finally trudging the rest of the way across the road.

Oliver heard Lynn let out a shaky sigh before she turned slowly to him.

"How... Tell me right now how you did that," she said. "The brakes were locked up. It wasn't going to stop."

Her widened eyes stared into his, and, for a second, he wasn't sure what to say. Her eyes looked like his father's when he saw Oliver cast fire magic for the first time. But she was different than him. She was fearless - or so it appeared when she confronted that guy who was about to beat the daylights out of him.

"Magic," Oliver whispered. "I told you before I-"

The pain on his chest began again, this time burning worse than before. He grunted as he ripped the collar of his shirt down as fast as he could.

"Oliver? Why is-"

He cried out again as the intensity - the fire - shot through his body. His fingers trembled as they pulled the skin from his collarbone down far enough for him to see... a second mark.

No, now they were forming together.

"Dammit," Oliver said, letting his shirt bounce back into place.

"Wow, I didn't know you could curse," Lynn said. "Let me see it."

Oliver shook his head as her hands came towards his shirt.

"No, it's-" her hand pulled the collar of his shirt down. "Please…"

"Shh," she said with a smile. "Is this a tattoo?"

His face heated as her fingertips grazed lightly over his chest. He didn't know why - and he couldn't even begin to think of an answer - he couldn't speak. Any time he'd try, his face would get even warmer.

"Oliver?"

"Um," he struggled to speak. "I-It's not a tattoo. I don't know what…"

He'd seen these markings before, but it had been so long he couldn't remember for sure. He knew he didn't see them on the boat… It wasn't that recent.

"I watched it move on your skin," Lynn said. "You don't know what it is?"

"No, I have no idea," Oliver shook his head. "But I've seen this somewhere in New Zealand."

Her fingers lifted from his skin, allowing it to return to its normal temperature.

"Okay, what's going on?" She put her fingers to her temples. "First the car, now this. What is this?"

"I-It's magic, Lynn," Oliver said. "That's how I stopped the car. But this…"

The mark on his chest was like the rest of his body. It wasn't carved or seared into his skin; it was as if it had been there his entire life.

"Magic's not real."

"Yes, it is. How else did I stop the car?"

If he'd known getting people to believe him about his magic was this hard, he would've left the ship years ago. Mr. Bain told him that people would instantly get angry and start riots, but even with proof staring this girl in the face, she didn't believe him.

"No, the brakes must have kicked in."

"Are you serious?" Oliver asked, and she shrugged. "How can I prove it to you?"

As she pushed her foot down on a pedal, moving the car forward once more, she tapped her chin thoughtfully.

"Well, driving on the road is annoying," she grinned. "Make the car fly and I'll believe you have… *magic.*"

"T-That's not how that works," Oliver said. "I can't just *make the car fly.*"

"Why not?"

He crossed his arms and stared at the carpeted floors for what felt like forever.

"Well. I don't know how."

"Mhm, mhm, thought so," she said.

Was… was this girl serious?

She just watched him set a leaf on fire, move a trash can without touching it, made a piece of paper levitate in his hand, and stopped a car without even having control over it. He knew he hadn't tried too hard to convince her that he had *actual* magic, but with the way Oliver's dad and Mr. Bain talked about it, he figured she would accept it immediately.

How far would he have to go before she actually believed him?

"Well, anywho, I'm pretty hungry. Why don't we stop for some gas and a bite to eat?"

If he could've rolled his eyes any harder, he would've. But instead, he nodded as she let out a teasing chuckle before punching him in the arm.

# Chapter 4

"Oh, I don't eat meat."

If there was ever a time that Oliver was scared someone's eyes were going to pop out, it was now. Lynn was *exceedingly* shocked. She looked the same way his teacher in grade school did when he 'somehow' got their soccer ball to stick to his nose without touching it.

"What in the name of God do you mean you don't eat meat?" Lynn asked. "Is that why you're skin and bones?"

*This* was more surprising to her than him stopping their car with his magic.

"No, I have a high metabolism," Oliver mumbled. "I just think it's wrong to…"

His voice trailed off as she took a huge bite from the burger in her hands.

"Sorry," she covered her mouth as he did his best to glare at her. "So, the food wasn't that much. We still have a good amount of money left."

"Money? Oh," Oliver watched her pull a wad of bills from her purse. "Wow, did you make all that working at the hotel?"

A tiny smile touched Lynn's lips as she stuffed it back into the large center pocket.

"Well," she said, her head bouncing from side to side. "I mean, I guess *technically.*"

"Technically?"

"My dad owed me money anyway. So, I went and got it from his safe. No biggie."

She took another large bite from her burger before sitting it back down on the plastic wrapping in front of her.

All his life he had been taught that stealing was wrong. Even his brother, who could use magic to do some crazy stuff, always told him not to take things that weren't his. But instead of being disturbed, Oliver found himself intrigued. Lynn took money from her dad's safe, and then they both stole a car. Not once this whole time had he seen even a little guilt from her. For that matter, *he* didn't even feel bad.

"Here, these aren't meat," Lynn said, shoving a small, paper bag in his direction. "They're potatoes."

"These... don't look like potatoes," Oliver said. "And they don't smell like potatoes either."

Again, Lynn's eyes looked like they were ready to leap from her sockets.

"They're French fries," she said. "Like, they cut them up and fry them, and then load them with salt. They're really good."

*"French* fries?" Oliver popped one in his mouth. "Like from France?"

"Maybe?"

They actually did taste heavenly. Maybe it was because he hadn't eaten since that morning, but those were probably the best potatoes he'd ever had in his life. His mom used to make them great when she baked them, but those were *amazing.*

"Hey," Lynn said. "I need you to be honest with me for a second, Oliver."

"Um, okay."

"That mark on your chest. You really don't know what it is?"

Oliver leaned his forehead against his palm, trying his best to think of where he remembered the distinct marks from. Could he have seen them on a statue somewhere in his village? On a sign going towards Greymouth? It had been so long since he'd been in New Zealand.

"I-I don't. But whatever it is, it's growing."

And the scariest part was that it was somehow enhancing his magic. He wasn't sure about that, but the last time he used the spell to stop something, it was weak and hardly effective at all. His power could've fed off of his adrenaline in the moment, but...

"That's not possible," Lynn said. "This is just about as ridiculous as you saying you have real magic."

"But I do," Oliver sighed. "Give me...like a coin or something."

Lynn opened her purse and shoved her hand all the way to the bottom. After a little bit of fishing, she pulled out a bronze colored coin and slid it across the table.

"I don't know what this is going to pr-"

"Watch," Oliver said, holding the coin in front of his face. As he removed his fingers from the coin, it stayed rigidly afloat. "Look, I don't know what magicians can do, but surely they can't do this."

Lynn's eyes narrowed as she studied it for several seconds.

"So, you can make a coin float but not a car?" She finally asked. "No way. I think other magicians can do that, too."

The coin fell to the table with a thud.

"Lynn, you said you saw the marks move earlier," Oliver said. "What more proof do you need that this isn't some trick?"

His voice was much harsher and louder than he meant it to be. In fact, he almost sounded angry, and he could tell he wasn't the only one that thought so.

Lynn's eyebrows pushed together, and her lips pursed in the same way a displeased guest's would on the cruise ship. He could also tell she was biting the inside of her cheek.

"Look, I'm not stupid," she said. "This isn't some movie or fantasy game. It's real life."

"Yeah, but-"

"No, you know what? If you're going to treat me like I'm stupid, I'm leaving," Lynn said, standing up. "You can use your *magic* to try, and stop me."

She hauled her purse off the table before she glared at him, spun on her heels, and made her way towards the door.

"L-Lynn," Oliver grabbed her hand before she could get to the door. "Please wait-"

"I'll be out in the car."

Her hand slipped from his fingertips as she pushed through the glass doors.

He sighed as he fell back into his seat. He knew living with magic was going to be hard - everyone told him so - but he didn't know it would be like that. Maybe he'd stop trying to convince her that he wasn't a magician. Nobody ever really seemed to want to know about it anyway. Mr. Bain told him not to use it on the boat, and even his mom and dad made him promise to never even mumble a spell. The only person who was ever okay with it was his brother.

His head fell into his hands as he squeezed his eyes shut.

It wasn't fair. All of those people were so mean and afraid, and the one chance he got to tell someone sweet and kind about who he was, he screwed it up.

"Dad, my back's itchy."

Oliver rubbed the moisture from his eyes as he looked towards the door.

A large, black man walked through the doorway with his son.

"Well, you were rolling around in the grass earlier. Let me see," the dad said, lifting up the back of his son's shirt. "Yeah, I can see it. Right here-"

*Yeah, I can see it. Right here.*

That was when it hit Oliver.

He remembered. He remembered where he'd seen the marks on his chest before.

*"Levi, sit still."*

*Oliver peeked around the corner of his parent's room and watched as his dad lifted the back of his brother's shirt. Levi had been complaining all week of a burning pain on his back.*

"Yeah, I can see it," his dad said. "Charlotte, right here."

*Oliver squinted his eyes and saw the black markings on his brother's back that his dad was pointing to. His mother squatted down, almost in his line of vision, and traced her fingers over it.*

"We knew this was going to happen," she whispered. "She said 'so lays upon this a curse of the prey.'"

"I know, but I didn't think it would come so soon," his father said. "It's going to attract more attention. And what with Macie having it, too."

"Oliver's the only one who's safe right now. He doesn't have it."

Levi had black markings on his back that were similar to what his was starting to look like. What did they mean, though? And what did his mother mean by he was the only one safe?

Oliver shook his head. He needed to tell Lynn.

If she was still out there.

He was almost too afraid to walk out those double doors. What if she wasn't there when he got outside? She could've left right then and there if she wanted to. And she probably did. She was so angry.

"I love you, too, buddy."

His ears perked as he turned his attention back to the father and his son. They looked so happy together. The son was all smiles as his dad picked up into his arms - giggling and cackling away as raspberries were blown into his cheeks.

Again, Oliver wiped his damp eyes as he pushed through the doors and out into the warm, summer night. He was staring down at the pavement as he walked out, and as his eyes flashed up, he saw the car.

"Hey," Oliver said, opening the door.

"Hey."

After he closed it, he stared down at his hands. His stomach was in knots, and the french fries were making him a little sick.

"Look, Lynn, I'm sorry-"

"No, I'm sorry," Lynn interrupted. "I lied to you earlier."

"Huh?"

Lynn sighed as she pulled her knees to her chest.

"I just shot up like, a week ago," she said, and Oliver tilted his head. "Like, heroin."

"But I thought you said you had enough when you almost got shot," Oliver said.

"It was definitely a wakeup call...for a couple of weeks," she whispered. "I just - I don't want to lie to you anymore, Oliver."

He inched closer and put his hand on her knee.

"Then don't."

The next thing he knew, she wrapped her arms around him and pulled him into a hug. He could feel, as he placed one hand on her head and the other on her back, that she was trembling. Her whole body shook as she exhaled a sob, and he couldn't help but pull her closer, just as his mom used to do with him.

"I'm sorry," her breaky voice said.

"Don't be," Oliver said, pulling away so he could see her face. "We're gonna get through this. I'll make sure of it."

Her brown eyes were puffy and wet - spewing out like a waterfall down her cheeks. He took his sleeve and grazed it over both sides of her face, smiling as she looked at him with a look of - he wasn't sure - but whatever it was, it made him feel warm.

"I promise," he said.

After a few minutes, Lynn had completely gathered herself, and she was once again level headed and even joking around. She teased him about not knowing what French fries were, and even slipped in a crack about him being a magician. He laughed along with her, knowing that in this moment, she didn't need to be convinced either way about his magic. She was laughing and happy again, and that was all that mattered.

"Hey," Oliver said as she turned onto a different road. "How do you know which way to go?"

"What?" Lynn asked. "My phone. I'm looking at directions on my cell phone."

Oliver looked down at the dimly lit, rectangular device sitting on her lap. He'd seen these on the boat, but he never got close enough to really look at one.

"Cell phone," he said, and it made a loud pinging noise. "What was that?"

"A message," she said, looking down at it. "What, do you not know what a cell phone is?"

He shook his head.

"What?" She almost yelled. "Like, a phone. You can call people and talk to them or send messages back and forth."

"Like people far away?"

"Mhm."

He stared down at it as it pinged again, illuminating the screen even more. It was blinding to the point where it was reflecting off the front window. He wondered if she could see through it better than he could.

"Do your parents ever worry about you, Oliver?" She asked suddenly. "Like, do you think they're thinking about you right now and where you're at?"

"Well, um," Oliver scratched his arm. "My parents aren't alive anymore."

She turned to him, her mouth agape.

"I'm sorry," she said. "I-I didn't know."

He stared out the side window and watched the trees, grass, and bushes fly by at an almost unreal speed. He wondered if Americans really got to appreciate everything around them. There were people going so fast that they were passing their car. Did they even notice all the trees or animals they were zooming past?

"How long has it been?" Lynn asked. "You know, since they…"

"Well, my mom, three years," Oliver said. "My dad about two. I can't remember too well."

The only one left alive in his family was his brother, and he didn't know where he was. Or maybe he wasn't even alive. It had been years since they had contact.

"Hey," Lynn said, pulling over. "I'm getting tired. Will you drive?"

"I- what?" Oliver's eyes grew wide. "Well… I can't drive."

"Come on," she whined. "Just for a few minutes. It's easy. Just hold the wheel straight with both hands, okay?"

His eyebrows creased together - almost in a Lynn-like expression, he noticed - as he nodded.

"Okay."

***

The road was getting bumpier than usual. It wasn't that bumpy when Lynn was driving.

He shrugged his shoulders as he continued on, softly humming a tune he always heard on the boat during the dinner hour. He always hated it when it came on, but since he hadn't heard it in a while, it felt like something was missing.

Another huge bump, that time sending his head against roof of the car.

"What the - Oliver!" Lynn said, suddenly awake. "Oliver, you can't just drive off the road!"

"But you told me to keep the wheel straight," Oliver said. "I don't know how to drive, I told you."

"What? Just get back on the road, dude! Follow the curves!"

His mouth twisted into a frown as she huffed, falling back into her seat when they finally got back on the road. She was mad, he guessed, but he wasn't too sure. She wasn't yelling at him or throwing things.

But still. The way she stared forward, eyebrows shoved together... the silence was making him squirm.

"Um, hey," he said, picking up a coin from in between their seats. He closed his hand around it, and then opened it up, revealing his empty palm. "Where'd the coin go?"

Out of the corner of his eye he saw a small smile twitch to her lips, and she shook her head.

He softly placed his hand on top of hers, and when he removed it, the bronze colored coin was sitting between the creases of her palm.

"How did you do that?" She whispered in amazement. "It wasn't even..."

He knew she wasn't going to like his answer, and for a second, he considered not saying it at all. But Lynn was doing her best to not lie to him, and he was going to do the same.

"Magic," he said with a smile.

"Yeah, yeah, but there's always a secret to the trick," Lynn snorted. "Come on... I won't tell."

Oliver rolled his eyes as he continued to drive.

He had that one coming. She was probably never going to believe him.

"Lynn, you said you weren't going to lie to me anymore, and I'm not either," Oliver tried one last time. "I promise you. It's magic."

He didn't have to look over at her to know she was staring him down. She didn't say anything, and he could hardly hear her breathing, so when he finally got on a straightaway, he glanced over. Her eyes were narrowed, and her head tilted.

"You're serious?" she asked.

He nodded his head slowly. It sounded like she actually believed him. He was nervous.

"So you really... have like, *magic*? Like, you can cast fireballs and summon thunder from the sky?"

Oliver put his hand over his mouth to stifle his giggle.

"No, not *that* kind of magic," he said. "Like, the stuff I've been doing. That's magic."

"So, you can't throw fireballs?"

"My brother can, but I can't. I don't know much about it to be honest."

He'd never really figured out what he could do. With his parents being so overbearing, he barely had time to practice and explore. Unlike his brother. When his dad sent him away, he probably had all the time in the word to practice his magic.

"If you actually have magic, why did you even ask me to come with you?" Lynn asked. "It's not like I can do anything, you know. I'm pretty much useless at this point."

"You're not useless," Oliver said. "You're inspirational."

She scoffed as leaned her head against the window.

"Whatever."

"Really, you are. Lynn, I was on that boat for three years." His grip on the wheel tightened. "And I was about ready to get back on it. You convinced me that I'm good enough; that I don't deserve the things they did to me."

"What do you mean?" She asked, sitting up.

That was something that he'd not thought about. After being on the boat - under Mr. Bain's control for so long - he'd forgotten what life was actually like. He forgot that sometimes you could have a break and a little fun. And most importantly, he had forgotten that he didn't deserve to be treated like an animal.

"Mr. Bain abducted me from my family when I was fifteen," Oliver said. "He threatened to kill my father if I didn't come with him. And I knew he'd do it, too."

"So you went with him," Lynn said quietly.

Oliver nodded.

"He didn't pay us - me and the other workers. Instead, he brought us to America and told us that if we didn't do what he said, he'd turn us in to your government," he continued. "I made him mad this one time. The very next day he told me that he had my dad killed. I-I... gave up after that."

"Oh my god," Lynn wrapped her hand around his. She turned his palm right-side up and traced his fingertips. "Did he... did he also do this?"

Oliver bit the inside of his cheek.

*The shattering sound was so loud that it caused the room to cease all conversation. Everyone was staring at him; looking him up and down and questioning his intrusion into their lives.*

*Oliver's lip trembled as he peered down at the broken plates scattered before him. It was his second day on cleaning duty in the ballroom - they'd never trusted him in there before - and he was already screwing things up.*

*"Hey!" Mr. Bain's voice tore his eyes from the mess. "What the hell was that?"*

*His mouth was dry, and as he opened it to speak, nothing came out.*

*Everyone's eyes were still on him, awaiting an answer of some sort. He knew if answered truthfully - said that he was rushing back and forth and misstepped because he was somewhat of a clutz - Mr. Bain would think he was being a smartass.*

*"I-I, um..." His teeth were mashing down on his tongue so hard he began to taste blood. "I'm sorry."*

*Someone in the crowd cleared their throat, and the quiet chatter returned around them.*

*"Someone clean this up!" Mr. Bain yelled into the kitchen. "Come here, boy."*

*As Mr. Bain's hand wrapped around his wrist, Oliver stared at their contrasting skin tones. Even though he was darkly colored, Mr. Bain's skin made him look almost white.*

*"Get in here," Mr. Bain yanked him into the kitchen and against one of the counters. "James, give me that."*

*Oliver's eyes flashed to James's, searching, begging him. But as he stared into them, he couldn't find anything. His eyes were black, one dimensional. They didn't even flash any pain or sympathy as he passed the large butcher knife over into Mr. Bain's hand.*

*"N-No, please-" the rush of adrenaline through his body tightened his throat. He couldn't breathe.*

*The rings on Mr. Bain's hand glistened in the light as they came down, and for a second, Oliver could see his reflection. But as the pain spiked through him, like thousands of tiny needles, his eyes flashed over to the severed tips of four of his fingers.*

*"Damn idiot," Mr. Bain said. "Wrap it. Get back to work."*

He shook his head in an attempt to shoo the memory away - to shove it back where it came from - but it made its way into his throat, feeling like a painful lump.

He remembered crying at the time, after Mr. Bain left, but that was two years ago. Why did still feel like that?

Lynn's hand squeezed his, easing the anxiety that had once again returned to his body.

"I'm-" his voice cracked as he fought back whatever sensation was starting in his chest. "I don't know what's going on, Lynn. But I need you to believe me, and I need you here."

He didn't want to cry. He hated that, and it made him feel worse than before. But his tears were trying their best to blow through the hard wall he'd work so hard to build over the past three years. They threatened to destroy and eliminate his sense of composure that he prided himself on while he worked on the ship.

"Pull over."

Oliver's eyebrows furrowed as he glanced over at her.

"What?" He asked, and she motioned him towards the side of the road.

He complied, pulling the car slowly into the grass so that the cars behind him, which had grown in number, could get around.

When all the lights disappeared, and the air around them had grown still, Lynn let out what sounded like a sigh, but could've also been a groan. Oliver wasn't too sure.

"You're telling me the truth? About everything?" She asked, and Oliver nodded. "About your parents, and this *Mr. Bain,* and... magic?"

"I-I am."

Lynn leaned back in her seat, staring out the front window towards the sky. He wished he knew what was going on beneath her thick, scrunched up set of eyebrows.

"God, both of us are pretty fucked up," she finally said, bringing a small smile to his lips.

He didn't know what it was about her, but she was so… charming. He'd never met anyone like her- someone so brash and brutally honest. Someone who said whatever came to their mind.

"But fine," Lynn continued. "You need me, and… I guess I need you, too. Whatever's going on here, we'll figure it out, and we'll get to New York. You and me, together."

"You mean it?"

"I mean it."

She motioned him with a stern finger to get out of the car and switch her spots. Thankfully, she was ready to drive again, because Oliver didn't know how much longer he could manage to squint his eyes.

"Alright, Abracadabra, we should find a hotel, because according to my phone you really drove us off course," Lynn smirked. "Closest town is New London."

"New London?" Oliver asked. "Like named after London?"

"Maybe?"

Oliver shrugged as he fell back in his seat from the acceleration of the car.

He was pretty sure Lynn believed him, but for some reason he felt uneasy. Maybe it was the marks on his chest, burning ever so slightly to remind him they were still there. Or maybe it was because he was scared that Lynn, after thinking about it for a while, was going to treat him exactly how everyone told him people would. Revealing his magic and her finally believing him should have been liberating, but things were never easy.

No, Oliver found that out the hard way many, many times.

# Chapter 5

"So, what do you think then?"

Oliver shook his head and rubbed his tired eyes, clearing up the image of the girl in front of him.

She stared at him expectantly, her arms crossed in a way that disrupted her tight, black braid from streaming down from her head and into her lap.

"Hey, are you listening?" She asked, slapping the back of his head. "What do you think of it? It just appeared last night."

Oliver's eyes followed her finger to the mark on her face. It was dark black, almost like someone had drawn it on her caramel colored skin with a marker. It started out in the center of her left cheek and swirled around the center once before it came out to singular, long tail that curled up past her cheekbone to nearly the corner of her eye.

"It's, um," Oliver shook his head. "What... is it?"

The girl let out an exhausted sigh before rolling her eyes.

"Uh, hello! It's the mark, stupid!" She said. "You know, the mark of the Cerva?"

Wait. That mark.

"The Cerva?"

"Do you pay any attention in class? You know, our tribe," she said. "The women keep their mark while the men get theirs burned off? Yours will be appearing soon. I heard it's pretty painful to get it burned off."

The girl was familiar, but he had no idea why. He'd never seen her before in his life. And the place - he glanced around, feeling like he was in a daze - he'd never been there before either.

"What does Cerva mean?" Oliver asked. "And who are you?"

"What are you-"

*A blaring horn cut through their conversation, and both of them had to cover their ears. It was low-pitched, and it vibrated not only the ground, but their entire body.*

"Kids, get up," *a man's voice said.* "It's the Lupus. You need to find a safe place."

"Where's daddy?" *The girl asked as she got up, pulling Oliver with her.* "Louis, tell me-"

*As Oliver breathed in the air, he could smell smoke. But there was something else, too. Something he couldn't quite name, but it brought his heart to a heavy pounding, and all the blood in his body felt ice cold.*

"Charlie, you need to get out of here," *Louis said, but she didn't budge.* "Boy, I need you to hide her. Leigh would be furious if he knew his daughter was in harm's way."

*Oliver opened his mouth, but that was when he heard it: the sound of screams. Ear piercing, agonizing screams of pain that rang through his head like a church bell at high noon.*

"There's a couple down there!"

"Charlie, get out of here!" *Louis said again, shoving the both of them towards the forest.* "Go! Before it's too late!"

*Charlie grabbed his hand, and before he knew it, they were running through the trees as fast as they could. He could make out the sound of rustling bushes and cracking branches around them, but she didn't seem to notice. She didn't even look back as they leaped over logs and splashed through puddles. Her hand, which was squeezing his tightly, was the only reassurance she needed that he was right behind her.*

"Aha! There they are!"

*Charlie gasped as they skidded to a stop.*

"What the-" *her voice choked off as four men came from the brush, surrounding them.* "Dammit."

"Thought you could outrun us, little does?" One of the men said.

She had her shoulders back and chest forward, but her death grip around his hand and her shaking arms betrayed her.

"Let us through!" She said, a tremble in her voice. "We don't want to have to hurt you."

"Let the chief's daughter go? I think not," the man said. "And I'd like to see you try to hurt me, kid."

Her hand released his, and as she thrusted it forward, Oliver could see a bright red begin to form in her hand. Before he could blink, or even figure out what was going on, a beam of fire shot from the palm of her hand, singeing the man in front of them.

Oliver's ears perked at the sound of more footsteps approaching in the distance

"Do you hear that?" Oliver asked. It sounded more like a herd now. "J-Just go, Charlie."

"What?"

"You need to get out of here. Your father, the chief-" the crunching leaves were louder. "You just need to go. I'll hold them off so you can get away."

Her dark green eyes began to well with tears, and she shook her head.

He didn't know this girl, he didn't know this place, and he sure as heck didn't know who these guys were, but he felt connected to them. All of them. Especially her. This black haired, green eyed, magical girl in front of him was special, and she needed to survive.

"Get out of here!" Oliver yelled at her. "I'll be fine!"

She spun on her heels and darted through the trees, but before she was gone, he could hear her voice call to him one last time.

"Be careful, Ollie!"

Ollie?

*There were hundreds of men around him, all shirtless except for the animal pelts wrapped around their waists. It might've been his imagination, but they all looked like they had red eyes and sharp fangs. And they were so all so tall, except-*

*There was a boy making his way to the front of the group. He looked familiar in the same way Charlie did.*

*"Eric, come see this Cerva boy before we kill him," the man in the front said to the kid. "Watch how he'll tremble and beg for mercy."*

*"I-I won't beg for mercy," Oliver dared to say. He didn't know where this newfound courage was coming from, but it was surging through him. "And I won't let you get to her."*

*The laughs from the men around him were more like growls of pleasure; as if they wanted him to fight.*

*"Can I do it, father?" The boy, Eric said. "I want to rip his arms off."*

*"No, son," the man said. "We need to save your first kill for the chief's daughter."*

*If Charlie was able to use fire magic, then he could, too. Right?*

*She just threw her hand forward and it came out. She said something under her breath. What was it? It sounded Latin, but was it?*

*"Come on, come on. Fire," Oliver said, and put his hand out. "Fire!"*

*The men in front of him laughed once again.*

*"The kid can't even use magic yet!" One said. "Pathetic. Alfie, kill him while we find the girl."*

*Oliver's heart skipped a beat. There was no way she had gotten very far yet. He had to do something. His brother taught him how to make a flame in his hand. Why couldn't he shoot a beam of fire?*

Come on!

*A small flame came to life in his hand.*

*Now he just had to extend that, right?*

*"Oh, what's this?" The man said, and the flame in Oliver's hand grew larger. "Maybe he* can *put up a fight."*

*The flame in his hand continued to swell until-*

*The pain from his chest ripped through him like serrated knife. As he looked down at the spot where the markings on his chest were before, the fire from his hand erupted, and everyone around him was engulfed in-*

Oliver couldn't stop the scream surfacing from his body as his upper half sprung off the couch. He tore the blanket from his body, hurling it across the room, and slapped his hand over the blistering spot on his chest.

"Oliver!"

Aqua blue filled his blurred vision, and as he blinked, he could make out Lynn's scrunched up, dark brown eyebrows.

"Hey!" She shook him by his shoulders. "What's wrong? What is it?"

After a couple of breaths to slow his heart down, he pried his fingers from the throbbing area. Lynn gasped and moved her hand towards the marks.

"T-There's more," she whispered, her cool fingers bringing relief from the ache.

"I… it's a tribal mark," Oliver said, trying desperately to remember his dream. "They can use magic, too."

Lynn's index finger traced the completed spiral. All it was missing was the long tail like… what was her name? He just said a minute ago.

"Is that what you were dreaming about? What's the tribe's name?" Lynn asked. "I can look it up the internet."

"Internet?"

"Oh, that's right. New Zealand." She put her hand to her head. "Just give me the name and we can get some information."

Oliver squeezed his eyes shut as he tried to remember what the girl in his dream said. All he could remember was running, fire… large men who wore animal pelts, the little boy who wanted to *rip* his arms off…

"I don't remember," he said. "We were running from a different tribe. They wanted to kill the chief's daughter for some reason."

"Okay, you know," Lynn said, handing him his blanket back. "I was looking at some stuff online, and apparently there's a really popular psychic in town. I think we should go to him."

"What's a psychic?"

Oliver slipped his shirt over his head as he watched Lynn's face change into an expression he didn't recognize.

"Well," she said, looking up at the ceiling. "They have these abilities and can interpret dreams and see people's pasts. And sometimes ghosts."

Oliver stared at her for what felt like forever, but she kept her eyes casually averted away from him. She looked down at her shoes, the wall, the ceiling again, her hands…

"Um, you know, Lynn," he said. "That sounds a lot like magic."

Her cheeks heated, and her lips scrunched together.

"I guess it does."

Oliver paused again.

"You've believed in psychics, but you didn't believe in magic?" He asked, and she crossed her arms. "Huh."

*"Huh?"* She glared at him. "What does *huh* mean?"

He shook his head as he covered his mouth, trying to hide his smile.

Lynn huffed and grabbed the remote from the television stand. The next thing he knew, it came flying towards him.

"Stop," Oliver whispered, and the remote froze midair. Lynn's mouth was wide open as she stared at it. "Nice try."

He felt his stomach begin to knot up as Lynn continued to stare, shocked. The remote fell to the floor, and he met her gaze, trying his best to read her dark eyes. After a couple of long, gut-wrenching seconds, she let out a melodic laugh.

"Well," she said, coming over and ruffling his hair, "you win this round, *Oliver.*"

He grinned as she made her way into the bathroom.

"Get dressed! We'll head out in the afternoon to go see this psychic."

He would admit that he was excited about going to someone to figure out what this burning mark really was on his chest, but that dream he had… it was just a blur. Would he be able to remember enough to have this person interpret it?

***

"Okay, we're next," Lynn said. "Don't be nervous."

The overwhelming smell of lavender filled the room, making Oliver wrinkle his nose. They used that exact smell in the bathrooms on the cruise ship, making him remember just that: the cruise ship.

He wondered if James or Mr. Bain noticed he was gone yet. They had to have. James would've brought it right to his attention. So why hadn't anything bad happened? It didn't make sense.

"Hello, welcome!"

Oliver pushed the beads hanging from the ceiling out of his way, revealing a tall, pale man sitting behind a table. He imaged a psychic would be dressed differently than this man, who wore a grey, buttoned up dress shirt - that matched his greying hair - black dress slacks, and black dress shoes.

"Hi," Oliver said. "Um, so how does this work?"

"Well, why don't you have a seat, Mister-?"

"Oliver," he said. "And this is Lynn."

The man reached out and shook both of their hands.

"My name's Grant," the psychic said, taking a seat, too. "Well, Oliver, Lynn, you seem to have brought a lot of stuff with you today."

Oliver watched as the man closed his eyes, breathing in deeply.

"I'm getting this aura from you, Oliver," Grant said. "You're stressed out about something that has recently come to. Is that right?"

"Yes," Oliver said. "I... for the past couple of days, this mark-"

"Wait," the psychic interrupted. "I'm getting something from a spirit nearby."

Oliver's eyebrows furrowed. He didn't want to seem like Lynn and be hyper-skeptical, but this didn't even look like real magic of any sort. His eyes drifted over to Lynn, and he could see she was staring back with an equally - and typical of her - aggravated look.

"No, I don't think there'd be any spirits-"

"There are always spirits, kid," Grant interrupted. "Here, give me your hand - both of you."

They both placed their hands in his before exchanging looks once more.

Oliver wasn't for sure what Lynn thought, but a few more minutes of this and he was out of there. It was turning out to be a joke. He would know - he *actually* had magic. This guy was a con artist of some sort.

"Yes, I'm feeling it more so now," Grant said, but then his face twisted. "A-Actually, I really do feel so-omething."

"What?" Lynn asked, trying to pull her hand away. "Hey, let go before I break your teeth."

Oliver tried to pull his hand away, as well, but the grip on his hand… it was like the girl's in his dream. It was tight and shaking, like he was scared of something.

"Be careful, Ollie," Grant said, his voice a higher pitch. His head twitched violently to the right. "Can I do it, father? I want to *rip* his arms off."

"What the fuck?" Lynn said. "Dude, let go."

"You know, the mark of the Cerva. The Lupus-" the psychic's voice choked off. "You can't escape. He knows. He knows. He knows. The seal. Break the seal."

Oliver could feel the burning on his chest reigniting, but no matter what he did, he couldn't pull away.

The next words out of Grant's mouth weren't English. They sounded like something the girl in his dream said as she casted the fire spell. But his was a long stream of tongues, and the more it went on, the more the mark burned. Oliver could feel it… *growing*.

"No," Oliver said, grabbing the man's arm with his other hand. "You're making it worse, let go-"

Grant froze in place for what felt like forever, but his death grip still held.

"Oh, Oliver," Grant finally said, opening his dark red eyes. "You can't cheat death again."

"What?" Oliver asked. "I've never cheated-"

"We made a mistake leaving you with Alfie," Grant said. "Eric will find you now that the mark has been revealed. There's no hiding. You can't get away, not again. Not again. Not again."

Oliver's head whipped to Lynn as he heard her gasp. He could see the grip around her hand was tightening.

"Oliver-" Lynn managed to say. "Do something!"

His eyes scanned the room for something - anything - and landed on a bowl in the corner of the room full of water. As he muttered under his breath, lifting the water from the container, he remembered that if he concentrated enough, like his brother taught him this one time, he could actually heat the it up.

"Eric will find you. He'll kill you. Kill you. Kill you."

"Oliver!"

Oliver flung the now boiling water at the psychic's arm, causing him to cry out and release Lynn's hand. Not even a second later, Lynn's foot went hurtling towards Grant's head, sounding a loud crack and sending him flying across the room.

Oliver grunted as one last sharp pain ripped through his body, sending him to the ground.

"Oliver?" Lynn said, bending down. "Oliver, what's wrong? Is it…"

She gently pulled the fabric away from his chest, revealing that the mark had grown. It looked like the girl's in his dream, except instead of having one tail protruding from it, there were four. One on the top, like hers, one opposite of it on the bottom, and one on each side. But the two on the left and right weren't black like the ones on the top and bottom; they were a dark red.

"Oh my god," Lynn said. "It's-"

"The Cervas - they won't last-" Grant struggled to say. "Eric will find y-you."

"That's the name of the tribe," Oliver said. "Cerva. That's what this mark…"

Grant began to stumble up, holding his head in his hands.

"You better stay the hell away," Lynn growled. "I can hit a lot harder than that, asshole."

The psychic was in a daze, swaying back and forth. Lynn's words didn't seem to register with him.

"Come on." Oliver took Lynn's hand. "Let's just get out of here."

He pulled the beads back for Lynn, making sure he kept his eyes on Grant as she passed through them.

"So lays upon this a curse of the prey."

Oliver froze in place.

"What?" He asked. "What did you say?"

"So lays upon this a curse of the prey. She tried to hide it after the Lupus killed everyone," Grant said into his hands. "But she failed."

Oliver shook his head as he backed towards the door.

"*She?* Who?"

"Charlie-"

"Oliver, come on!" Lynn yelled. "Leave the freak alone. Full of bullshit."

Oliver stared at Grant for a couple more seconds, a shiver running down his back. His heart was pounding, and his veins were pumping with adrenaline. It took every bit of strength he had to tear himself away from the shaking man.

"Hey," Oliver said when he stepped out of the door. "Are you alright?"

Lynn's arms were crossed, her eyebrows were pressed together, her eyes were wild, and as she stared up at him - she looked like she was about to cry.

"What's going on?" She whispered.

"I don't know," Oliver said. "Something happened a long time ago, and it's just now catching up."

*So lays upon this a curse of the prey.*

That was what his mother said to his father when they saw Levi's mark on his back. How did this psychic know that? For that matter, how did he know all the things said in Oliver's dreams?

Charlie, Eric… the Cerva and the Lupus. What did this all mean, and what did it have to do with him?

"Let's get back in the car," Oliver put his hand on her back. "We have the name of the tribe now, so we use that internet thing to look it up, right?"

Lynn nodded, her face still scrunched up in what he could only imagine was anxiety. He knew how she felt. The deeper they got into it, the more lost they seemed to get. His father never seemed to want to talk about magic, and that might've been why. He didn't want to get in too deep.

But… Oliver couldn't help but wonder what secret lie awake on the other side of the seemingly endless pit they had just entered. He had to keep going.

# Chapter 6

"So it says that the *Cerva* was a tribe of nature-loving, New Zealand natives that used live near Mount Victor."

Oliver's hands tightened on the steering wheel as he went around yet another sharp curve. He wasn't sure whether the anxiety he felt was from driving, the angry drivers passing him every ten seconds, or the anticipation of figuring the mark out.

"A lot of people avoided them and the mountain, it says, because of rumors of witchcraft," Lynn continued. "The women are best identified by the spiral marking tattooed on their body. The men, however, lack this mark so as not to be identified by enemy tribes while hunting."

"So that means…" Oliver started. "Why would I have this mark?"

Lynn shook her head as she ran her finger up and down on her phone.

"I don't know, but - oh! Here's some more info on the mark," she said. "The mark is usually done in black ink, one tail for each family member, but sometimes some of the tails are red, meaning-"

Lynn bit her lip and closed her eyes.

"What?" Oliver asked. "Why are they red?"

"T-They… well, when the tails of the mark are red, it means-" Lynn scratched the back of her head. "Each one symbolizes a dead family member from that tribe."

That didn't make sense. Oliver was beginning to think that maybe he had this mark because *he* was a member of the tribe, but there were only four tails on his mark.

"There were five in my family. Me, my dad, my mom, Levi, Macie," Oliver said. "My mother and little sister were killed, and my father was later. Levi's still alive, I think."

"Then… your dad? He wasn't a member of the tribe?"

His mom and sister were dead, which meant they were the two red marks. Levi was probably alive; he was intelligent enough to stay out of trouble and hide. That left him and his dad, but one mark.

"Well, no, no, this doesn't make sense," Oliver shook his head. "My mom didn't have magic or the mark."

"Not that you knew of," Lynn said. "You had to have gotten it from somewhere."

Oliver's mouth twisted into a frown. It'd been so long since he last saw his mother, and he was having trouble remembering her in detail. She always kept nearly every inch of her skin covered. Even the makeup she wore was caked on her face at all times.

"What else does it say?"

"It says that they were pretty much wiped out by an enemy tribe called the Lupus. The Lupus get a mark of their own for each person they kill from the same immediate family," Lynn said. "If they complete the mark and eliminate all family members, they go to heaven celebrated or something."

*Wait.*

Oliver turned on his turn signal and pulled off the road.

"Oliver?"

*"Strip him down and check again. I don't believe his father."*

*Oliver wiggled his toes on the cold, wooden floor. It had been an entire day since they snatched him from his home and dragged him onto this ship, and not one time had they said anything directly to him.*

*His clothes were once again stripped from his body, and he was spun around in a circle, every inch of his body inspected.*

*"Sorry, Mr. Bain, sir. Nothing."*

*"Dammit," the man, Mr. Bain, said. "Just when I thought I finally had it."*

*Oliver's eyes drifted around the cabin as he wondered why they brought him there. If he didn't have what they were looking for, why did they take him?*

*"Where's your brother, boy?" Mr. Bain said, but Oliver kept quiet. "Are you deaf? I can kill you, too, you know. It's no skin off my nose."*

*"I-I... he left home a couple weeks ago," Oliver whispered. "What... Where's my mom and sister?"*

*Mr. Bain laughed as he smoothed his brown bangs from his eyes.*

*"They're another tally on my board, boy," he said. "I just need your brother."*

Mr. Bain was looking for something that his brother, sister, and mother had... and he didn't at the time.

His little sister, Macie, shortly after she was born, was forced to wear long sleeves and gloves even during the summer. Levi was never allowed to take his shirt off when they were playing outside. His mother was always hiding underneath layers of clothing and makeup.

"Oliver?" Lynn said. "What's wrong?"

The mark on his chest felt heavy as he became overly aware of its presence.

They all had what he didn't: *the mark*. And Mr. Bain was trying to kill everyone in Oliver's immediate family that had it. His dad lied to Mr. Bain and said Oliver was adopted because he wasn't sure if the mark had appeared.

"Mr. Bain is a Lupus," Oliver finally said. "That was why he killed my mother and sister and was looking for my brother. They all had the mark of the Cerva."

"But now you have it," Lynn said. "Does that mean-"

"He's going to be looking for me now, too."

Both of them were silent, the only sound filling their ears were the passing cars and the humming of their own vehicle. Oliver couldn't even hear breathing.

"Lynn," he started, turning to her. "This is… not something you probably accounted for when we left Massachusetts."

She shook her head.

"I guess what I'm trying to say is that I guess I have a lot of baggage that I didn't know I had," he continued. "And I'll understand if you don't want anything to do with it-"

"The fuck do you mean?" Lynn interrupted. "I'm not going to abandon you. Is that what you're suggesting?"

Her eyes glared at him with a burning far worse than the mark on his chest gave off, leaving him speechless. She crossed her arms and her eyebrows slanted drastically.

"Well," Oliver said, averting his eyes away from hers. "Lynn, if he finds me, he'll kill me, and if you're anywhere near me, he'll do the same to you. I don't want that."

"I'm not leaving you."

She didn't understand. She didn't know Mr. Bain like he did. One little slip up on the boat was enough for Mr. Bain to have his father killed. If she was going to be with him, trying to hide him and protect him, he'd kill her just for the fun of it.

"I'm not going to put you in danger-"

"This isn't your choice, Oliver. It's mine," Lynn said. "You didn't leave me when I told you about my drug problem. You promised me that we'd get through it. And I'm promising you the same."

Oliver wanted to argue with her, but her stern scowl told him that he wouldn't get anywhere. She was more stubborn than anyone he'd ever met in his life. As charming as it was a majority of the time, it was different. It was going to get her killed.

"Okay, I guess," he sighed. "So what do we do now, then?"

"New York," Lynn said, and Oliver gave her a funny look. "What? The plan's still the same. If that guy comes anywhere near us, I'll beat the shit outta him. How's that?"

It wasn't that simple. Oliver wasn't sure whether or not the Lupus were able to use magic, but even without it, Mr. Bain was a force to be reckoned with. If he was able to keep someone as big and built as James on the ship, he had to have something up his sleeve.

But he wasn't going to challenge her. He was beginning to learn that when Lynn wanted something, she was going to get it. And she wasn't about to leave him.

The thought, even though somewhat stressful, also gave him comfort.

He was no longer alone. Not anymore.

\*\*\*

The mark on Oliver's chest was long forgotten as he stared wide eyed at the buildings around them.

"Wow," he said. "This is New York?"

"Mhm."

The buildings were huge. Some had glass tops, some had large fences surrounding them. There were people shoulder to shoulder on the streets, walking fast or moseying along as they stared down at their phones.

As he rolled down his window, the smell of fried food from the trucks nearby filled his nose and made his stomach growl so loud that it made Lynn giggle.

"How about we get something to eat, then?" She asked, and he nodded. "I guess I'll try and find a vegetarian friendly place."

"It's okay. Pick somewhere you like, and I'll find something," Oliver said, watching all the people bustle by.

Lynn pulled into a parking spot on the side of the road.

"Be careful getting out, cars here-"

A loud horn sounded as Oliver stepped out and closed his door. The car it came from was slowly inching forward, waiting to get around Oliver.

"Hey! Get the hell outta the way before I run you over!"

"Stop," Oliver whispered, and the man's car immediately bucked to a halt.

He felt Lynn's hand on his arm.

"Oliver. Don't, uh, don't do that," she said, pulling him to the side walk. "New Yorkers are kinda mean."

"Like *you* mean?"

"Well," she laughed. "Maybe more."

Oliver noticed, as they strolled down the sidewalk, that she hadn't let go of his arm. She hung on it, since she was so short, forcing him to take smaller steps so she wouldn't fall behind.

"Have you ever had popcorn before?" She asked as they neared a food truck. "It's just corn."

Oliver shook his head, and the expected, surprised look fell on her face.

As Lynn ordered it at the window of the food truck, one popcorn and one hot dog, Oliver couldn't help but pick up the tense atmosphere around him. He looked around for what could be causing it, but the scene was the same everywhere he looked: people in hats on their cell phones walking briskly past on another. Was it the remembrance of the mark on his chest that was causing him such unease?

He rubbed it through his shirt. It wasn't aching, but he was still painfully aware of it. The fact that his mother was a Cerva, and she and his dad had been trying to hide it for so long blew his mind. The only question he had was why his own mark took so long to appear? Levi got his when he was nine, and Macie got hers when she was only a year old. Why had it taken him eighteen years to get his? That psychic was saying something about *breaking the seal*. What did that mean? Why would his be *sealed* and Levi and Macie's not?

"Oliver?"

His eyes came back into focus as he realized the voice that said his name wasn't Lynn's. He was staring forward into the eyes of a boy about his age. Tall, pale, blonde hair, cuts and scars on his face -

"Karp?" Oliver asked, realizing it was one of the other workers from the ship. "What are doing here?"

"What is it?" Lynn asked. "Is someone bothering you?"

Karp turned on his heels and began walking further into the alley behind him.

"No, he's another worker on the boat," Oliver said, taking a step forward. "I don't know why he's…"

"Hey, wait," Lynn held him in place. "Haven't you ever seen the movies? This could be a trap, you know."

"What?"

Karp was getting to be well out of sight now, meaning Oliver had to make a decision.

"Come on," he grabbed Lynn as he ran across the street.

They walked down through the dark pathway, Oliver only faintly able to see the back of his ex-coworker. Soon, though, they came to what looked to be the opening to a courtyard. Karp had turned over his shoulder to make sure they were following right before stepping into the brightly lit opening.

"Karp? Hey." Oliver pulled Lynn into the opening with him. "What are you doing here?"

"Oliver," Karp said, his hands in his pockets. "You need to come with me."

The look in his friend's eyes was not one he recognized. Much like Oliver, Karp was one of the only workers on the ship that was not quite *optimistic*, but more positive than the rest. James and a couple of others who had been on the ship for a while were hardened and emotionless, but he and Karp were always trying to see the best in things.

"You got off the boat?" Oliver said. "Does Mr. Bain know? How many others escaped?"

"No, you don't understand," Karp said, his face still solemn. "Mr. Bain's the one who sent me to find you. You have something he wants."

Oliver's breathing had grown shallow as the realization hit of just how easy it apparently was to find him. If Karp was able to hunt him down that fast, then it would take Mr. Bain no time at all.

"I don't know what you're talking about," Oliver said, playing dumb. "What does he want?"

"That mark coming from your chest. It's the mark of the Cerva, isn't it?" Karp asked, and Oliver's eyes narrowed. "Mr. Bain isn't sure how your mother knew how to seal it away as well as she did, but it's broken now."

"Oliver's not going anywhere," Lynn said, stepping forward. "I don't care who this *Mr. Bain* is."

Karp's eyes drifted over to Lynn, and he stared at her for a good minute with his frost colored eyes. It was enough to make Oliver shiver, but Lynn didn't seem to be bothered by it in the slightest.

"I don't know who you are, dear," Karp said, pulling his hand, as well as a small handgun from his pocket, "but this doesn't concern you."

*That* was enough to scare some sense into her. She froze in place, and her tough face faltered.

"Karp, don't," Oliver said. "Put it away."

"Come with me or I'll shoot her," Karp said, pointing it towards her. "If I don't bring you back, do you know what Mr. Bain will do?"

He didn't know specifically what Mr. Bain would do, but Oliver was sure he could think of a number of things.

"This kid's full of shit, Oliver," Lynn said. "He won't shoot."

"You wanna bet?" Karp asked. "It's my life or yours, and I don't know you."

"Karp. No."

Oliver's eyes widened as he watched his friend's finger pull back on the trigger, which then sounded a loud bang. He knew he wasn't going to have time to react, but as he turned his head, he could see a tiny, silver bullet flying in slow motion through the air.

Oliver inhaled deeply, mustering up every ounce of strength - every little bit of magic he could feel in his body before he threw his hand out.

"Stop!"

He could almost feel the magic rush from every limb in his body, and then explode from his fingertips.

There was silence. Dead silence as the three of them stared breathlessly at the bullet floating inches from Lynn's forehead.

"I-I..." Lynn choked out. "I..."

"You used *magic!*" Karp said, dropping the gun. "You can't use magic!"

The clink of the bullet falling to the ground echoed off the walls of the courtyard.

"Get out of here, Karp."

Karp's eyes widened as he stared up at Oliver, tears in his eyes. "What-"

"I said get out of here," Oliver growled.

Karp took a step backwards as a small flame began to burn in Oliver's hand. It grew bigger and bigger with each passing second as Karp's skin became paler and paler.

"*I'm* the one who has what you and Mr. Bain want," Oliver said, stepping towards Karp. "If you ever try to hurt her again, you won't be getting away without a scratch."

"O-Oliver, he'll kill me if I go back without you," Karp whispered. "He said so."

Oliver's eyes drifted to the ground. Karp was the closest thing he had to a best friend while they were on the ship, but he couldn't go. Lynn would never let him, and if he did then *he* would be the one to die. He had to choose between his own life or Karp's.

"Then don't go back," Oliver said. "But you need to leave us. Now."

Karp backed up a few steps before turning and running, not even sparing a glance back before he was gone.

"You... stopped the bullet," Lynn said. "How did you catch it that fast? I was so sure that I was-"

Oliver watched as a tear rolled down her clammy skin.

"Lynn, no, it's okay," he said. "He's gone."

He could see her arms, which had been frozen in the same spot since Karp pulled the trigger, were now shaking. Her breathing was ragged as she inhaled deeply. It was all too much for her; all the magic and the tribes. He had warned her, though, and even gave her a chance to leave and forget about it all.

"You can leave anytime you want, you know," Oliver whispered. "I know it's a lot…"

"I'm not leaving you." Her voice was less sure than the last time she said it.

"Then let's go, okay?" Oliver took her hand, and her fingers wrapped around his reflexively. "Let's go get a hotel room. It's been a long day."

It *had* been a long day.

But it was only the beginning, Oliver knew, of what Mr. Bain had in store for them. He didn't know whether or not Karp would run away or report back to Mr. Bain, but either way he was going to find them. It was only a matter of time, and he had to be ready.

Maybe he couldn't protect himself, but he needed to protect her.

## Chapter 7

"Hey, Lynn."

Lynn noticed, as her eyes came back into focus, that she'd been gazing out the window for what felt like forever. Actually, when she looked over at the clock, it'd been about twenty minutes. She wasn't thinking about anything specific, but with Oliver watching the tv screen in awe, she found her mind wandering and trying to process the events from the day.

"You know how I have real magic, so I'm not actually a magician?"

Lynn stared at him for a second, and then laughed at how ironic that sounded.

"Okay?"

"Well, I think I've got a magic trick that will fix that," he said, and grabbed a blanket from the bed. "You wanna see?"

When she nodded, he got up and ran to the doorway of the room. He then held the blanket against the frame, covering his entire body. Well, almost his entire body. She didn't know if he noticed, but he was so tall that she could still see his toes wiggling with excitement on the other side.

He pulled the blanket down for a second so she could see his grinning face.

"Now you see me," he said, pulling it back up over his face. She watched as his feet turned and quickly tiptoed behind the wall before the blanket fell to the ground with no one behind it. "Now you don't!"

His face appeared around the door after a couple of seconds to look at her reaction.

It would break her heart to tell him that particular trick had already been all over the internet for the last two years, so she put her hands over her mouth and feigned surprise as much as she could.

"Cool, right?" He asked. "I think that'll be my first trick when I become famous."

It was crazy to her how relaxed he could be after what had happened. Maybe it was a coping mechanism that had carried over from the ship. He might've learned a way to keep his stress under control even in hostile situations. Not that they were in a hostile situation at that moment.

Her eyes drifted back over to Oliver to see that he'd gone back to watching the show. It was about four guys who played uncomfortable pranks on each other for fun, and she could see he was entirely absorbed, even when they did the most cringy things.

"What do you want to do with your life?" Oliver asked suddenly.

"Oh," Lynn inhaled deeply, giving the matter some thought. "Well, like, I've always wanted to go to college. Dad said we never had enough money, though. Probably because all the drinks."

He was quiet for a while, and she could almost *see* his brain working.

"Well, you will," he finally said.

Lynn raised her eyebrows at him.

"What?"

"When I make it big as a magician, I'll pay for it," Oliver said. "I'll pay for you to go."

The goofy, lost look on his face had all but vanished in this moment.

"Why would you do that?" She asked. "We don't really even know each other, Oliver."

Oliver turned the television off and got up to sit down close beside her on the leather couch. He pulled his knees up to his chest and stared down at the floor for a while.

"You changed my life," he said, and wrapped his hand around hers. "I want to do the same for you."

They had formed the habit, she'd noticed, over the previous few days. She'd never been a big one for hand holding when she dated in high school, nor had she been huge on falling in love. Normally she'd date the guy who she knew had the biggest stash of whatever she was using at the time and give him a go until she got tired. She thought she was going to be the same way with Oliver. He'd given her a sense of adventure and excitement, and even though the magic of running away from home was wearing thin, she wasn't ready to give it up. For the first time in her life, she wanted to see someone through.

But... would it cost her?

"Um, are you okay?" Oliver asked. "You don't look well."

People always say that love makes you do crazy things. Was emotion clouding her judgement? Was this situation like all the others? Something dangerous she needed to get away from but was still too blind to see?

"Lynn," Oliver poked her arm. "Hey, Lynn."

"No, I'm fine," Lynn said, squeezing his hand. "I was just thinking."

"About what?"

Did she really care so much about this boy she met not even a week ago, that she was ready to risk her life for him? She was sure earlier when she met that other boy from the boat, but since she'd had time to process it...

"About how tired am," she said, staring into his dark green eyes. It was a relief that with all these magic powers he had, mind reading wasn't one of them. "Let's go to bed."

Oliver nodded as he got up to pull one of the pillows from the bed, as well as the comforter.

"Actually," Lynn said. "You can, um, leave those there."

"I'm just trying to make the couch more comfy to sleep on is all," Oliver said. "It's better than the beds were on the boat, but it's still a little hard."

Lynn bit her lip as she shook her head. "Well, what I mean is that you can sleep on the bed," she paused, "with me."

Oliver's cheeks heated from their regular tan to a light pink, and his eyes fluttered. He didn't say anything as his gaze went from the bed to her twice.

"Are you sure?" Oliver asked, and Lynn nodded. "Well, okay."

As Lynn pulled the blankets up, Oliver slid in next to her, but as close to the edge of the bed as he could get. As she peered over at him, his face was a dark red and his eyes stayed to the ceiling.

"You can get closer, you know," Lynn said. "I don't bite."

Oliver scooted closer, bridging the gap between them enough for Lynn to feel his body heat and the wool from his long-sleeved shirt he was wearing.

"This is really comfy," Oliver said. "I don't think I've ever had a bed this nice."

Lynn's heart sank. She couldn't imagine what he'd been through all his life. Especially the previous three years.

"Don't you normally sleep without a shirt?" She asked.

"I-I, um, yeah," Oliver said. "But I didn't think it was appropriate for me to...um."

"You can. I don't mind."

Oliver sat up and slowly pulled the shirt over top of his head. She could see, as he turned to throw it off the bed, that his back had several pale, faded scars. His arms, which were skinny, but also curved and built in places, also had them littered all the way down to his elbow. As he twisted forward to lay back down, she saw the mark.

The tail coming off the top curved up to his collarbone, the two red ones on the sides stretched out one to his arm, the other to about the middle of his chest, and the one on the bottom traveled all the way down to his breast.

"Lynn?" Her eyes flashed up to his. "Are you sure this is okay?"

She nodded as she turned her head back to the ceiling.

"Good night."

She felt Oliver turn on his side as he turned out the light.

"Good night," Oliver said, and then added softly, "thanks for staying with me."

Lynn wasn't sure if he meant for her to hear it, so she pretended like she didn't as she closed her eyes and waited with open arms for a dark, peaceful slumber to fall upon her.

\*\*\*

Oliver listened closely, hearing Lynn's even breathing. It had taken her forever to fall asleep, and he couldn't help but think it was from his presence in bed with her. He made her nervous, for some reason, which then made him nervous. If he would've left his shirt on, it probably would've been less… awkward? Was that the word? He wasn't for sure, but with the drowsiness creeping up on him, he didn't have much time to think before he was drifting off.

*"How did you do that?"*

*Oliver's eyes fluttered open as he once again saw the face of the Cerva chief's daughter.*

*There were others around him, too, staring at him with wide eyes. Louis was also there, but half of his arm was gone, and the stub was wrapped tightly with bandages.*

"Ollie, how did you make it back?" Charlie asked. "There were hundreds of them when I ran."

"I don't know, I..." Oliver's eyes went down to the mark on his bare chest. "I think it was this."

Charlie turned to Louis, and he nodded.

"His mark must have appeared when he was casting magic," Louis said. "Looks like it appeared at just the right time. You wiped out a good chunk of their army."

As his eyes scanned the area, he noticed there were only about twenty people around him. Had only this many survived? How could the Lupus be this powerful?

"It made my magic more powerful?" Oliver asked, receiving another nod. "And the Lupus. Do they have magic, too?"

"Some of them do," Charlie said. "But all of them have the power to track a family of Cerva once they've killed one."

"That's why it was good you allowed Charlie to get away," Louis said. "This new child they have is out for her and her father. If they got her, they'd be able to track the chief."

The woods around them was quiet, the only sound was the quiet breathing of the people surrounding him.

"Chief Leigh!"

Oliver turned his head towards the hillside as a man descended, hand on his side, limping as quickly as possible.

"Daddy!" Charlie said. "Daddy, are you alright? Someone help him!"

Several people rushed towards him, catching him just before he began to fall forward. He let out a grunt, but then lifted his head towards his daughter with a weak smile.

"Take me to her," he said, and the people brought him forward. "I'm so glad you're okay."

*"I wouldn't have gotten here if it wasn't for Ollie."* Tears rushed down Charlie's face as she hugged her father tight.

*Leigh picked his head up once more, this time looking at Oliver. He signaled him over, and Oliver complied, getting up and slowly shrugging past a couple of the adults standing between the two of them.*

*"Ollie, thank you," he said, putting a hand on top of Oliver's head. "Thank you for saving my Charlotte."*

Oliver nearly threw himself out of bed as he awoke.

His skin was clammy, he noticed, as he yanked the covers off and got up. He paced the room back and forth, hand to his forehead as he tried to calm himself.

*Charlotte?!*

His *mother* was the chief's daughter! And that made him the Cerva chief's *grandson*. But what he couldn't figure out was who this person was that he was playing in the dream. They kept calling him *Ollie,* something only his brother ever called him, and, after, looking down at his mark during his dream he knew he was in a body other than his own. The mark looked familiar to him in his dream, but it only had three tails on it, not the four that he had.

God, when Lynn found out -

Oliver's eyebrows creased as he realized that he hadn't seen Lynn since he had gotten up. He should have already noticed her presence, and by now she would've already been over asking him what was wrong. But she was…

He poked his head in the bathroom - nothing.

Just for the hell of it, he got down on his stomach and checked under the bed… but she wasn't there either.

"Lynn?"

He didn't know why he called for her. If she wasn't around, she obviously wasn't going to be in earshot. But where could she be? His eyes roamed the room, seeing that her purse, coat, shoes, and clothes were gone. The only trace left of her was the wrapper and cup used for coffee.

His butt thudded on the bed.

Maybe she'd finally come to her senses and realized just how much she was risking by staying with him. He'd told her twice that she could leave whenever she wanted, and he was ready at both moments for her split, but this time… there was this sinking feeling in his chest and stomach.

His fingers drummed on the mattress of the bed as he realized he didn't know what to do. The plan was once they got to New York, he was going to try to make it big as a magician somehow. Then, once he got some money rolling in, he'd help Lynn enroll in college, like he promised, and then everything would be okay. Mr. Bain would probably show up, but at that point Oliver would have everything together enough for Lynn to be okay when he was gone.

He was on his own.

He wasn't sure whether or not he was still going to try the whole magician thing. Sure, he loved practicing his magic in front of everyone and seeing all the amazed reactions, but that would only draw attention to him. It would probably be best if he laid low while Mr. Bain was looking for him. He'd be willing to risk his cover for Lynn so that he could help her like she helped him, but not for himself.

No, this didn't make sense. Just the day before, she said she wasn't going to leave him. She was extremely intelligent, and if she was going to come to her senses, she would've already done so. Something had to have happened to her.

His stomach twisted as the thought of Mr. Bain once again entered his mind.

What if he'd gotten her?

Oliver pulled his shirt over his head and headed out the door, urgency in each step he took. There was no telling what Mr. Bain would do to her, and if he hurt her like he'd hurt Oliver then...

He didn't know what he'd do. Part of him was still terrified of even the vague thought of Mr. Bain, but the other part...

He shook his head. She probably went out for a walk is all. There was no way he got her.

\*\*\*

As he roamed the streets, shrugging past slow tourists or musicians camped out on the sidewalk, Oliver's eyes scanned every nook and cranny he could find. He'd circled the block around the hotel at least fifty times, and he hadn't seen her. She could've gone inside, he thought, but with how fast he was moving, there was a slim chance he missed her.

The smell of fried food once again filled his nose, and the streets became busier. It was lunch time, meaning he'd spent a little over an hour outside looking for her.

Oliver noticed, as he stood frozen in the middle of the sidewalk, that his heart was starting to race. His muscles felt tight, especially around his chest, and he was mashing his teeth together. His fists were clenching, and for a second, his vision became blurry.

She was *gone*.

The mark began to burn again, and soon enough, a pain ripped through his chest, causing him to squeeze his eyes so tight that-

*"I finally found you, Miss Charlotte."*

*Oliver's eyes widened as he saw the Lupus boy, Eric, looming in front of him. Except he looked older - and as Oliver looked down at his own hands, so did he.*

*"Ollie, just run!"*

*He turned, and he saw Charlie - his mother - behind him. She was standing aggressively in front a black-haired man who, as Oliver looked closer, was clutching a small child in his arms.*

*"No," Oliver said, feeling a sudden burst of courage. "No, I'll protect you."*

*"You're going to protect her?" Eric asked. "Last time we played this game you almost lost. Do you really want to chance that again?"*

*Oliver cracked his neck to one side as he tried desperately to remember whatever it was he was talking about.*

*"Honey," he heard Charlie whisper to the man behind her. "You and Ollie take Levi and run, okay? As fast as you can. Don't stop."*

*Oliver's breath caught in his throat as he took another look at the baby behind him.*

*That was... Levi. His brother.*

*"Charlie, you go with them," Oliver said. "I'll take care of this guy once and for all, and then I'll catch back up, okay?"*

*"But you-"*

*"Go."*

*The shuffling behind him slowly began to fade until he could no longer hear it, leaving he and the Lupus boy alone.*

*"It's crazy to me that you'd risk your life for someone who doesn't even have anything to offer you," Eric said with a chuckle. "Let me through, and I'll spare you."*

*"You're not getting her," Oliver said. "I'll make sure that you-"*

*His voice choked back as he felt his skin beginning to rip apart like the worn seams of a shirt. When he looked down, he saw Eric had lunged forward - he hadn't even see him move - and stabbed him in his chest.*

*He coughed, sending a glob of dark blood onto the ground-*

"Move outta the way kid."

Oliver's eyes came back into focus as he was shoved out of the way of a large man as he walked past. It took him a second to remember where he was and what he was doing, but he soon remembered Lynn.

He needed to look somewhere other than the block directly around the hotel, but New York was so big. She could be anywhere; nearly impossible to find. And with this pain he was feeling in his chest, every jostling movement made him wince.

Oliver jogged across the street and into a small alley. If she was hiding for some reason, it'd probably be in one of those small spaces. She was tiny and could fit in a lot of crevices back there.

"Lynn?" He called out into the open space.

If she heard his voice, she'd come out. He'd protect her from whatever was either after her or whoever took her.

He spent the next several hours doing this same thing over and over again. He'd find alleyways, which were abundant, and call her name. Each empty echo back towards him made his heart sink lower and lower, until finally, the sun was setting, and he was somehow back where he started.

His stomach growled as new scents of food refreshed his sense of smell. It wasn't something that was new to him - he was hungry all the time on the boat with what little they fed them - but the craving for food mixed with the confusion he was feeling made his stomach ache harder.

*One more time.*

He had to check around the block one last time.

His swollen, heavy feet began to trudge down the same sidewalk again, but then skidded to a stop as his eyes locked on a path he hadn't seen earlier. He knew that he didn't have anything to lose, so he forced his legs that way.

It was a scenic path that reminded him a little of his home town. There were lots of shrubs, flowers, trees, little squirrels playing, and-

"What are you doing here?"

Oliver's eyes lifted from the ground and his heart skipped a beat.

"Lynn!" He said, closing the distance between them with a hug. "I didn't know where you went, and I thought that maybe you-"

When he pulled back to look at her face, he noticed one of her eyes was squeezed close. The closer he looked, he could see that the area around it was a light grey. As he wiped his finger across it, rubbing the makeup away, it was a darker purple.

"Hey, quit!" Lynn pulled her face back.

"What is this?" Oliver asked, holding onto her firmly. "Is your - did someone *punch* you?"

Her thick eyebrows creased together as she tried to tug away from him, but her attempts were weak, almost already defeated.

"Come on, Oliver. I just wanna go back to the hotel."

"Who hit you?" He asked. When she didn't answer, his voice got louder than he meant. "Lynn, who hit you?"

She chewed her lip a couple of seconds before looking back up at him.

"I... okay, I went to go buy some stuff-"

"What *stuff?*"

"I-I needed some junk, okay? My mind was racing with all this magic shit going on," Lynn said. "And then this asshole overcharged me, and I called him out and then, well, you know."

Oliver gazed into her deep, brown eyes as he raked his brain for what exactly he should say to her, but his mind came up blank. He could feel his face heating and his lips pursing together. His eyes narrowed as he thought about someone rearing back and punching her hard enough to bruise her.

"Where's he at?"

"What?" Lynn's eyes widened. "Oliver, I just want to go-"

"Take me to where this guy's at," Oliver interrupted. *"Now."*

He was surprised at his tone. He was beginning to sound less like himself and more like the person he'd been playing in his dreams. The strong, confident, protector that was... his opposite.

Lynn's arms fell to her sides as she motioned her head forward.

Her eyes were on the ground as they walked, making Oliver want to reach out and grab her hand. But he held back. If he faltered any, she would try and talk him out of finding this guy, and he wasn't having that.

The path led to a park area with a fountain in the middle. With the sun setting in the distance, reflecting off the water, Oliver could barely see the man leaned up against the stone fountain wall Lynn pointed to.

"Hey," Oliver said, walking towards the man. There were other people around, but he didn't bother to keep his voice down. "What the hell do you think you're doing?"

The man, who was caught off guard by Oliver's abruptness, was easy to lift off the ground as Oliver's veins coursed with adrenaline, and his hands filled with the soft material of the man's shirt.

"What the-"

Oliver let go of him, and the man's back hit the stones with a thud.

"Oliver, stop!" Lynn said, but he ignored her. "Oliver!"

The man stood up, dusting his coat off for a couple of seconds before glancing first at Oliver, and then Lynn.

"So, you came back with what?" He asked. "Your boyfriend?"

"What the hell gives you the right to hit her?" Oliver growled. "You too scared to pick on someone your size?"

The man laughed as he looked Oliver up and down.

"And you're my size?" He said. "Don't waste my time, kid."

Without thinking, Oliver threw his fist forward, hitting the guy's nose, and sending him backwards into the fountain. Oliver noticed the conversations around the park had grown quiet, and there was a crowd of people around them.

"Okay, you made your point," Lynn said, grabbing Oliver's arm. "Let's go back-"

"You brat," the man said, and as he swung his fist forward, Oliver whispered under his breath. The water from the fountain shot up, encased his arm, and then froze solid. "What the fuck?"

Oliver then jumped up on the fountain wall, right next to the man, and launched his fist at him again. He could hear a cracking sound this time as the man fell back into the water.

"Oliver, we need to go now. Stop!"

As he stared down at the man, who was holding his head as he cringed away, it was almost as if something - reality, maybe - hit him in the side of the head.

He had just used *magic* in front of everyone; just like he did in Lynn's dad's hotel. Except this time, no one was looking at him in amazement. They were staring up at him in horror. With wide eyes. They backed away as he turned to them.

"Hands in the air!"

Oliver watched as six men came pushing and shoving through the crowd of people. As they neared him, they pulled out their guns, pointing them straight at him.

"Hands. In. The. Air."

Panic washed over him as his arms lifted slowly, and his eyes went to Lynn.

Three of the men ran to him, the other three to the guy in the water. He was soon thrown roughly to the ground, his hands cuffed behind back.

"Suspects in custody."

Oliver was lifted painfully to a standing position and forced forward towards a red and blue flashing car. The people around him parted for an easy path forward, and soon began dispersing per the orders of whoever was yelling.

When they got to the car, he was shoved into the back.

He had no idea where he was going, but he had a feeling he was in deep trouble.

# Chapter 8

Oliver continued to sit silently across the table from the scruffy, large, smelly man in uniform. His badge, Oliver eyed quickly on the table, said the word *police* on it. He looked down at his wrists, which were still cuffed together with cold, metal handcuffs.

"So, boy," the man said, making Oliver flinch. "Where are your papers?"

"My what?"

The man sighed as he leaned forward onto the desk, looking at Oliver like the answer was obvious.

"Your papers. You know, the things that say you're allowed to be here?" He asked, and Oliver shook his head. "You don't have papers, huh? So how did you get here?"

"A-A ship."

The officer continued to stare at Oliver, looking him up and down, looking at his hands, his face, his neck where his mark was peeking from underneath his shirt.

"You came here on a raft of some sort? I don't know if you-"

"No, a ship. A cruise ship," Oliver interrupted, and the officer wrinkled his forehead. "I was a worker on a cruise ship, and it left me behind."

"And you didn't think to wait for it?"

Oliver's eyes went back to the cuffs around his wrists and he stayed silent.

He wasn't sure how much he could tell this man. Chances were he already saw Oliver use magic. If he found out much more, what would he think? Would Mr. Bain be right when he said that the American government would do horrible things to him if they found out?

"Sir," another man came in. "His description fits the one of the missing worker filed in Massachusetts. Oliver Lee."

"Well, looks like you're telling the truth," the officer said, rubbing his finger against his greying mustache. "But you just committed assault. And over drugs, no doubt."

"No," Oliver said. "It wasn't over drugs."

The man laughed, both of his hands holding his stomach as it shook.

"Bullshit," he said. "Do you know how much heroin and cocaine that man had on him?"

"No?" Oliver wrinkled his nose. "He hit my friend, so I hit him."

Oliver heard the jumbled static of the radio strapped to the officer's chest.

"Hold on," he said into it, and then pointed his fat finger in Oliver's face. "Stay here. Don't move, don't talk... I don't even want to hear you cough. Understand?"

Oliver nodded his head vigorously.

As the man made his way out of the room - well, *waddled* was really the right word - Oliver could feel sweat beginning to pour from his forehead. He didn't know where Lynn was, and apparently there was a missing report out for him. No doubt from Mr. Bain. And there was a new issue, something about *papers* and *assault*. He was only trying to protect Lynn.

His fingers drummed on the desk for a couple of seconds before he remembered what the officer said and curled them into a fist so as to keep the temptation away.

When the door behind him finally opened, and he turned, he was met with another unfamiliar face.

The tall, built, blonde haired man held a file in his hand, and wore a baggy, beige coat that went a little ways past his waist. He was the polar opposite of the officer that was just here.

"Well, well," the man said, taking a seat. "Oliver Lee, huh?"

"Um, yes, sir," Oliver said. "Who are you?"

The man's eyes lifted from the paper, a hint of surprise in them.

"Huh. That's not something I hear a lot," he said. "The name's Nik Rafiel. Ring any bells?"

"No," Oliver shook his head. "Sorry."

As Nik lowered the folder from his face, Oliver could see his amusement. His grin, which consisted of only half of his mouth turned up, the other still in the same place, was actually comforting. Oliver didn't know what he said that was funny, but at least someone in here didn't have something against smiling.

"No, no, it's fine. You're from New Zealand. All's forgive," Nik said, laying the folder on the table. "I was there when you got into that fight with that guy. Pretty brutal stuff."

Oliver flinched as he realized what was coming next. They were about to talk about how in the name of God he was able to lift water and freeze it to that guy's hand. He was already in enough trouble and judging by this man's confident aura he gave off, it appeared he already knew something. So, lying was out of the question.

"Yeah," Oliver said quietly.

"Let me just cut to the chase," Nik said. "That was probably the best magic trick I've ever seen. And that's saying something, because that's exactly what I do for a living."

"You're a magician?"

"Sure am!"

Wait, if this guy wasn't a police officer, what was he doing here in the room? Oliver's eyes went to the tinted window that took up nearly the entire side of one wall, then to the door, and then back to Nik.

"You can get out of those, can't you?" Nik motioned to the handcuffs. Oliver nodded slowly. "Show me."

During the whole ride to the station, Oliver had been thinking about just that. The cuffs had ridges on the inside, locking them into place tightly around his wrists. But as he whispered under his breath, smoke slowly began to rise from the tiny keyhole. He twisted one of his wrists to the side, and the metal piece - newly smooth instead of serrated - slid out, freeing him. He did the same with the other.

"Incredible," Nik whispered, yanking his finger away after touching the warm metal. "How did you do that?"

"I, um," Oliver's fingers twisted together before he looked up. "Magic."

Nik stared at him intently, making Oliver shrink back into his seat. For a couple of seconds, he wished the other guy was in there instead. But after Oliver had sunk far enough down into his chair, Nik's cheery laugh filled the room, bouncing off the walls.

"A magician never reveals his tricks. Smart kid," Nik said, and then shrugged his shoulders. "Why don't we go ahead and get you outta here, huh?"

"What?" Oliver asked. "How?"

"Well, here's the deal, Oliver," he leaned back. "I got a show I'm doing here next week, and my opening act just dropped out. If you agree to fill that spot, I'll get you out of here."

Oliver could hardly believe what he was hearing.

"You can do that?"

"You can do anything when you've got enough money, kid," Nik laughed. "What do you think? You on board?"

Oliver's mind went back to Lynn. This was what they were planning, but she was nowhere to be found. He wasn't sure if they arrested her, too, or if she was waiting back in their hotel room.

"Is Lynn here? I don't-"

"You mean the little, blue haired girl that was yelling at you in the park?" Nik asked. "Yeah, no, she's here."

"I'm not leaving without her."

Nik grinned as he stood up to stretch. First to one side, then the other, and then he leaned forward and put his hand behind Oliver's ear. When he pulled it back, in front of Oliver's face, there was a small, copper coin between his fingers. Oliver's eyes widened as Nik dropped the coin on the table.

"You drive a hard bargain, Oliver," he said. "But you've gotta deal. Be back in about twenty minutes, okay?"

***

"Oliver!"

Lynn's arms wrapped around his neck as she pulled him into a tight - almost too tight - hug. She was struggling to reach, since she was so short, so as he hugged her back, he lifted her up to his height.

"Alright, alright, you're happy to see each other," Nik said from the door. "Let's get outta here. Police freak me out."

"Is that-" Lynn's eyes bulged. "Are you Nik Rafiel?"

"See, kid," Nik said. "That's the reaction I'm used to."

Lynn's head whipped around to Oliver, and for the millionth time - he didn't know why his lack of knowledge still surprised her - she looked at him like he'd said something crazy.

"Oliver, you didn't know who *Nik Rafiel* was?" She asked. "He's only *the* best magician in the United States. What are you doing here?"

"Well, I just happened to see some unfound talent," Nik said, putting his hand on Oliver's shoulder. "He's going to open for my show here in New York."

Lynn's eyes went back and forth between Oliver and Nik, but Oliver didn't need to ask to know exactly what she was thinking. She was wondering if Nik knew that Oliver had *magic,* or if he thought he had... 'magic.'

"Isn't that great?" Oliver said, giving Lynn a reassuring smile. "And then after that I can start performing for money-"

"You know you're not doing this gig for free, right?" Nik interrupted, and then rolled his eyes. "Forgot to mention. The pay's pretty okay. How does ten thousand sound?"

"Is that a lot?" Oliver asked, and he saw Lynn put her hand to her forehead.

Nik laughed as he motioned his hand in the air at a taxi.

"You're a riot, Oliver," he said, opening the door for them. "For you, it's a lot."

As they climbed in, Oliver first, Lynn in the middle, and Nik next, Nik spouted off an address to the driver, and they were off.

"Is that enough to go to college?" Oliver asked, and Nik wrinkled his nose. "Lynn wants to go."

"Yeah, not with that drug problem of yours, you don't," Nik said, and Lynn's eyes went to the floor. "Well, I'll tell you what. If you kick that nasty habit, I'll go ahead and pay for a semester at NYU. With the way Oliver does magic, he'll be able to pay for the rest."

Oliver grinned as he watched Lynn nod.

"Do you think I'll be able to make that much?" He asked.

"Kid, I know you will," Nik said. "You're going to be big."

The excitement welling up in body was enough to make him pop. Oliver couldn't believe it, but everything was actually going to be okay. Sure, Mr. Bain still sat on the back of his mind, but, at the moment, his name was but a distant memory. As he, Nik, and Lynn talked about the coming week, James faded from his mind, Karp, the cruise ship, the mark of the Cerva, his dreams… all stored somewhere safe. Something for him to worry about another day.

He was ready to put it all behind him; to try and live free from his and his family's past for a while. Whenever the day came when he'd have to worry again, he'd take it one step at a time.

# Chapter 9

Oliver's heart was racing as he exited the stage, the cheers and screams from the crowd pumping his body full of adrenaline. He came around the curtain and was met with warm, brown eyes and a tender smile.

"Here," Lynn said, handing him a water bottle. "You have everyone freaking out back here. They have no idea how you do any of your tricks."

"Damn right," Nik said. "How the hell did you make that coin float so far from your hands? I didn't see *anything!*"

Oliver grinned, making Nik roll his eyes before making his way out onto the stage for the main performance. He tried not to do anything too incredibly out there yet. He wanted to warm everyone up to it, and plus he didn't want to make Nik look bad.

"Why don't we go to your dressing room so we can-" Lynn's voice cut off as Oliver stumbled backwards. "What's wrong?"

His chest was burning again, and as he stumbled his way to his dressing room - out of sight of the crew members - he ripped his black jacket and white dress shirt off and threw it to the ground.

"Why's it doing this?" Oliver groaned. "I don't understand."

He fell backwards onto the couch in the room, hand over his chest like he'd just been shot.

"It's okay," Lynn said. "I've got you."

The loud humming of the fan was the only thing he could hear, though. Its drone note was almost trance-like, and with the pain from his chest, his thoughts began to swim in his head. He couldn't concentrate on just one. And then, old memories - ones that he hadn't thought of in years - started surfacing and mixing in.

There was one that stuck out, though. One that rudely shoved its way right in front of his eyes.

"There's no other way, honey."

His mother's melodic voice filled his ears from the other room, and he was rushed with a feeling of nostalgia as he realized he was sitting in his old home. He glanced out the window and saw that it was dark out, meaning that he should've been in bed. But for some reason-

"Charlotte, you can't," his dad said. "What about the kids?"

Oliver peeked around the corner and saw both of his parents. It had been three years since he was taken and seeing them there ... his eyes were damp.

"If I do this, there won't be a chance at all that he finds us," his mom said, and Oliver noticed the knife in her hand. "He can't track the kids if I kill myself. It'll ruin everything for him."

"We're far away, though, remember? We ran," his dad whispered. "You said it'd be hard for him to find us if we were far away from him."

His mother pulled the knife back, but his father had already grabbed her arm.

"You can't do this, Charlie," he said through clenched teeth. "You can't do this to me!"

"Let go!" His mother said. "I'm trying to save you!"

"Just drink this, Oliver."

Cold liquid touched his lips, causing his eyes to burst open. He pulled away as quickly as he could, causing the water to spill all over his torso.

"O-Oh," Oliver said, realizing he was back in his dressing room. "Lynn?"

"I'm here."

Oliver's eyes met hers once more as she took a seat beside him. Her fingertips grazed his skin before lying flat against his chest. Their cold touch once again brought him relief as he let out a sigh.

"Hey, Ol-" Nik's head popped in. "Am I, uh, disturbing something?"

Lynn popped off the couch, her hands up in the air as she back away from Oliver.

"N-No, of course not!" She said and crossed her arms.

"Right. Oliver, you're trending," Nik said, holding out his phone. "And I just got a call for you to go to an interview on this one lady's show."

Oliver tilted his head.

"Trending? What's that?"

"What-" Nik put his hand to his head. "Right, New Zealand. People are talking about you on the internet! Like, a lot of people!"

"Oh. Good things?"

Nik nodded so enthusiastically that the microphone taped to his cheek fell off.

"This is just the start, kid," he said. "Soon, everyone'll know your name."

Oliver shook his head. Everything was happening so fast. How was it all happening to him? Just the other day he was scrubbing food up off the floor and taking people's plates back so he could wash them later that night.

"Congratulations, Oliver," Nik said, winking. He then disappeared back around the door.

With a sigh, Oliver leaned back into the couch.

Things were actually okay.

***

Oliver's eyes went to the television as he heard his name and saw that his interview from the day before was on. They pre-recorded it because he had *another* interview he had to go to that day. Nik had been lining them up for him since the performance, and even though it was only week four of his 'journey to stardom,' as Nik called it, he was already exhausted.

"How do you do it? I don't understand!" The woman said, leaning back in her chair. "Show me again."

Oliver watched himself once again lean forward, place his hand in front of her nose, and pull a coin out thin air - almost like it came from the inside of her nose.

Everyone around him gasped, and the lady put her hand over her forehead. Her eyes were wide in amazement, and like she'd said backstage, this was the moment she almost fainted.

"I'm telling you guys, I'm right here and it just comes out of nowhere!" She said faintly. "So, we'd like to get to know you a little bit more, Oliver. We know you're a great magician but tell us where you're from. Tell us your story."

"Well, I was born in Haupiri, New Zealand, in the Christian community of Barak," Oliver said. "It was a really secluded place, but we managed to be self-sufficient."

"How did you get here? In America?"

Oliver watched his shoulders tense up as he took in a deep, calming breath.

"I was abducted, after my mother and little sister were killed by a man who forced me to work on his cruise ship for three years before I was able to get away..."

He turned the television off before he could hear anymore. He didn't like the sound of his voice on tv. It was foreign - which Nik said was perfectly normal. Still, though, he knew how the interview went. He talked about his life, and what it was like for him and his family to constantly be on the run. Of course, he couldn't say exactly the truth about why they were on the run, but a man chasing after them seemed to be sufficient enough for every interviewer. He left out the details of what it was like growing up with magic, and, instead, filled them in on how the experience of living in a strict Christian community was. He talked about how his brother left when Oliver was only eight years old, but he didn't dare tell them it was because Levi got caught teaching him magic. All these details he was leaving out were such a big part of his life, and it was almost as if he was lying to them-

A sharp knock on the door drew him from his trance, making him realize he had been staring at a black screen.

He looked over at the alarm clock on his side table. It was only about two o'clock, way too early for Lynn to have gotten out of class.

His smile grew as he thought about Lynn being at college. They were so fortunate that Nik paid for her entire first semester, and with the money Oliver had earned from the shows the two of them were doing, he had saved up enough for the last three years she had to go. However, just yesterday he'd purchased a storage unit and safe to put it in. He didn't know enough about banks to be suspicious of them, like Nik was, but it was per Nik's suggestion. Also, Oliver never knew when something might happen to him when he-

Another knock, more urgent.

Oliver slowly tiptoed his way to the door, squinting through the peephole.

*What?*

All the air in the room disappeared as he saw a tall, black man dressed head to toe in a neatly pressed suit. His arms were crossed, and his left black dress shoe tapped impatiently on the ground as he waited outside the door.

"No," Oliver whispered, and Mr. Bain's eyes went to the peephole.

Oliver backed away, holding his head in his hands.

"I know you're in there," the voice outside the door said. "Get out here."

His mind raced as he shook his head.

*I want to rip his arms off.*

As he fell back on the bed, he heard the door click and swing open.

*Last time we played this game you almost lost. Do you really want to chance that again?*

"Well, well," Mr. Bain said. "We meet again."

Oliver's eyes were wide, his hands still on either side of his head as Mr. Bain squatted down, reached forward, and tipped Oliver's chin up.

Neither of them said anything, and Oliver couldn't look away from Mr. Bain's brown - almost black eyes.

"Adopted my ass," Mr. Bain chuckled. "You have your mother's eyes."

His mother.

Oliver's fingers twisted in his own hair, and through clenched teeth, he muttered under his breath. The next thing he knew, water - from the bathtub he hadn't drained yet - came flying through the air. It hurled itself at Mr. Bain's feet, freezing the instant it came into contact with him.

But Mr. Bain didn't even flinch. He held Oliver's chin with authority, not letting up any pressure as he gazed down at his feet.

"You're going to have to do a lot better than-"

Oliver muttered under his breath again, sending a shard of ice from the floor towards Mr. Bain's face. It sliced through his cheek, continuing its way up towards the ceiling before Oliver lost control of it, sending it back on the ground.

With his other hand, Mr. Bain wiped his cheek, observing the red skid mark it left on his black skin.

"L-Leave me alone," Oliver dared to say.

Mr. Bain's eyes went back to his as he grabbed the collar of Oliver's shirt and pulled it down. A hum filled his throat as his middle finger reached forward, tracing the shape of his mark.

"Do you want me to tell you how I killed her, boy?" Mr. Bain whispered, paralyzing Oliver. "Or should I tell you about your sister?"

"N-No," Oliver choked out.

His finger stopped on the left tail of the mark, and with each tap against Oliver's chest, the red color seemed to deepen.

"Your poor sister," Mr. Bain said. "She barely had enough time to cry before I shoved my knife through her."

"Get away…" Oliver shook his head. "P-Please."

"I can still remember how slowly the life faded from her eyes," his finger went back to the center of the mark, and he followed it up to the tail on the very top. "Now we have you. I wonder how long it'll take for yours to fade?"

"I-I said get away!" Oliver shoved him, the ice shattering as Mr. Bain fell backwards.

That was when he took off as fast as he could. He darted through the door and was soon stomping down the stairs.

They both knew that this time was going to come. But with all the interviews and shows and Lynn's semester starting they'd pushed it to the back burner. How could they have been so stupid? The mark on his chest was a literal reminder of the impending trouble.

As soon as he burst through the door and outside, he turned and mumbled under his breath. The door, much to his surprise, caved in a little, making it to where it couldn't be opened. He had no idea how he did that, but he didn't stick around long enough to think much about it.

Oliver knew what he had to do.

*Let go! I'm trying to save you!*

Mr. Bain was going to catch him, and Oliver was going to die. He had no doubt of that. But there was a way to end this game of cat and mouse. Maybe not for him, but for his brother.

*If I do this, there won't be a chance at all that he finds us.*

But he needed to find Lynn first.

Oliver didn't know how he managed to run the entire way to Lynn's university - he'd put on a few pounds since Nik found him - but he soon found himself running past signs for academic buildings.

How was he ever going to find her, though? There were so many people and buildings.

His eyes went to the clock tower to his right. It was only three o'clock, way after lunch time. He couldn't remember when she said her classes were, or when she got out.

Each minute that ticked by with him standing there made him sweat even more. Mr. Bain could be anywhere. Watching him, stalking him, getting ready to-

Aqua blue caught his eye, and as his head whipped around, he saw her.

"Lynn!" He called, and she stopped in place. "Lynn."

"Oliver? What the hell-" her eyebrows pushed together as she made her way over to him. "You were just on the tv. How'd you do that?"

"I-It doesn't matter," Oliver said, shaking his head. "Look, we have a problem."

With the light the way it was - reflecting off of her autumn eyes - he almost felt okay again. But his brain kicked him back into focus, and the adrenaline rushed through him.

"What-"

"Mr. Bain just showed up at our apartment," Oliver forced out. "He's looking for me, Lynn. He saw my mark and he's going to…"

Lynn's face was even paler than usual as her lips parted, and she struggled to speak.

"W-What do we do?" She asked. "He's not going to kill you, I won't let him-"

"Lynn, this is going to be my life. No matter what I do to dodge him, he's always going to be there," Oliver interrupted, and then slapped a key in her hand. "Here. I've drained all the money from my bank account and placed it in a safe in the storage unit just down the street from our apartment. No one knows about it, and this is the only key."

His words were rushed and panicked, but as he wrapped her fingers around the key, his touch was gentle. Her hand was so soft and warm that he couldn't help but linger like that for a second - his hand wrapped around hers, staring into her eyes...

"Why are you giving me this?" She whispered. "Where are you going?"

"I said I would pay for your college, and I'm going to," he said. "But... I-I gotta go, Lynn. I *need* to go."

"Oliver-" he pulled away from her, backing up slowly. "Oliver, please, we can figure a way out of this."

He shook his head, matching her step towards him with another away.

"I have to go," he said again softly.

Before she could say anything else - before she could even begin to stop him, he was far away from her.

"No, Oliver!"

# Chapter 10

Oliver's lungs were like fire as he raced up the stairs, holding onto the railing for support. He didn't need to turn around to know that the thudding behind him was still the same thing as it had been for the last six flights of stairs.

His legs pulsed and the muscles in his stomach tightened even more as he turned up the next flight. He didn't know how much longer he could go, but he could see the door. If he could just make it that far, it would be a flat and smooth run from then on out.

As he neared the door, he whispered under his breath, sending it flying off its hinges and out onto the rooftop.

"Stop!"

He spun around just as he got to about the center of the roof and was met with a hard kick to the chest, sending him rolling. As he struggled to pick himself up, he could hear Mr. Bain's chuckle getting louder.

"Give it up, *boy,*" Mr. Bain said, his foot slamming down on Oliver's chest. "This ridiculous chase has gone on long enough."

Breathing was already hard enough after the kick, but with the weight of his foot slowly crushing Oliver's chest, it was as if he couldn't get anything in.

"S-Stop, you can't-"

"I should've known your mother sealed your mark away," Mr. Bain almost growled. "I should've known you were hers after I heard your name. *Oliver.* You tricked me for a good three years, didn't you?"

With the last bit of strength he had, Oliver forced arm up towards Mr. Bain.

"F-Fire," he said, and just like in his dream, the flame in his hand grew. "Fire!"

Mr. Bain barely pulled back fast enough as the beam of fire exploded from Oliver's hand.

Oliver pushed himself from the ground. His legs were shaking, and it took him a couple of seconds to steady himself before he met the glare of his former captor.

"What do you mean after you heard my name?" Oliver asked. "I don't understand."

Mr. Bain rolled his eyes.

"That brat that followed her and her husband around for years. *Ollie,*" he growled. "He was a pesky little thing. Until I finally killed him. He was the only reason she lasted long enough to have you and that brother of yours."

If it hadn't been for this *Ollie* guy, Levi, their dad, and their mom would've gotten killed. Oliver would've never even been born, and neither would his little sister. It was all because this one guy pledged to keep her safe.

But for what?

*It's crazy to me that you'd risk your life for someone who doesn't even have anything to offer you.*

For the sake of the tribe?

"So then... now what?" Oliver said, shrugging his shoulders. "I'm here. You're here."

Mr. Bain walked towards him as he took his jacket off, revealing a mark similar to Oliver's carved into his arm. But instead of the tails coming from the swirl opposite of each other, they all came off one large, central trunk. And they were all red.

All except for two of them.

"Well, now I'm going to do what I should've done three years ago," Mr. Bain said. "You know, your mother's plan was flawless. She renounced Cerva soon after Ollie died, meaning that none of you would've gotten the mark. But then your father had to jump in my way, and she made a deal to save him."

"A deal?"

"So lays upon this a curse of the prey," Mr. Bain laughed. "That's what you've been your whole life, Oliver. The prey. And I've been your hunter."

Oliver's eyes widened as he saw blue appear in the broken doorway.

"Oliver!"

He cursed under his breath as she ran towards them, but she was jerked back her father, who Oliver couldn't imagine clearing all those flights of stairs.

"Just get out of here, Lynn," Oliver said, his eyes going back to Mr. Bain.

"Let go!" she tried to pull away. "Let go! He's going to kill him!"

"Honey, he's not going to kill him," he could hear Mason whisper.

Oliver backed away slowly towards the edge of the rooftop until he felt his legs hit the ledge, but Mr. Bain continued to come nearer.

He jumped up onto the ledge, dangling his heels over the side and causing everyone to freeze.

"Get off!" Lynn screamed, finally pulling away. "Oliver, don't! Don't do it. Please."

Oliver gazed longingly at her. Her short, blue hair had grown out a little since they got there, and he could see her blonde roots beginning to show at the top of her head. Her eyes, which were welled up with tears, held a sense of passion in them, unlike when he first met her. Her face didn't have that scrunched up, bored look on it anymore, either. She'd really changed.

*He* had really changed.

As he picked his foot up, his body began swaying back and forth.

"Oliver! Don't!"

For the first time in three years, he was feeling things again. The sorrow, the pressure... the happiness. He had forgotten what happiness was until he met Lynn. And after his mother and father were killed, he had forgotten what love felt like.

But that was before he met her.

He stared down at his foot for a long time, watching how it struggled to hold his body weight up. He knew Lynn was still screaming, but all of his concentration was on his toes; the only things that were between him and the roadways below.

"Sleep," Mr. Bain said, and Oliver watched both Lynn and her father fall to the ground.

"W-What did you-"

"When we're done here, I'm going after your brother," Mr. Bain grinned. "I think since you both have given me so much trouble, I'll make him suffer a little before I kill him."

Oliver's breath caught in his throat as he thought about his brother.

For the longest time, he believed Levi was dead. Everyone else in his family was, so why would his brother be any different? He knew his brother was slick and could get himself out of anything - he always did when they were kids - but death was different. Death seemed to want to ruin all parts of Oliver's life.

But then he saw the two black tails coming from his mark; that was the first time in a long while that he'd been sure that his brother was still out there.

"Maybe I'll cut him open and let him bleed out," Mr. Bain continued. "He'll be the last catch, after all. I want to make it count."

He couldn't let his brother die. Not after everything he'd been through. He deserved to live a normal life.

"You're not going after him," Oliver said. "Not if I ruin your game of catch."

Mr. Bain crossed his arms.

"You're not going to do that," he said. "You're like your mother. Scared of death. You should've seen her groveling at my feet right before I killed her."

Oliver lowered his foot back to the ground.

"That's right," Mr. Bain said with a chuckle. "Besides, if you tried that, I'd just -"

Oliver threw his hand forward, sending the wind full force past him, and launching Mr. Bain into the air. And then, as it died down, letting up the pressure on Oliver's own back, everything around him began to rush past, like when he and Lynn were in the car together. But this time, everything was sideways.

He couldn't hear much as he fell weightlessly through the air, but what he could hear was that tune again. The one they played at dinner time as the guests arrived in the grand ballroom of the massive cruise ship. He hummed along with it once more as he closed his eyes.

He no longer hated the repetitive melody that rang through his head. It didn't fill him with the same stress and tension it did before when he prepared himself for the busy night.

Instead, he felt relief spread through his body as he realized that both he and his brother were free from the shackles of their past.

Megan Ransdell is a wielder of magic and darkness. She builds worlds only to tear them down piece by piece, mountain by mountain, all for the enjoyment of –

Okay, she's actually an author, but what's the difference?

Megan enjoys writing fantasy and has an especially soft spot for creating magic heavy worlds. In order to keep her magic powers a secret, she has cleverly disguised herself as a college student working towards her B.S. in Psychology.

In her free time, she enjoys spending time with her family, painting, doing yoga, and trying to figure out what exactly makes people tick. *Now You See Me* is her debut novella.

Made in the USA
Columbia, SC
21 May 2022